88

REASONS WHY
AUSTRALIA
IS THE

Craziest

SIMON CRERAR

ABC Books

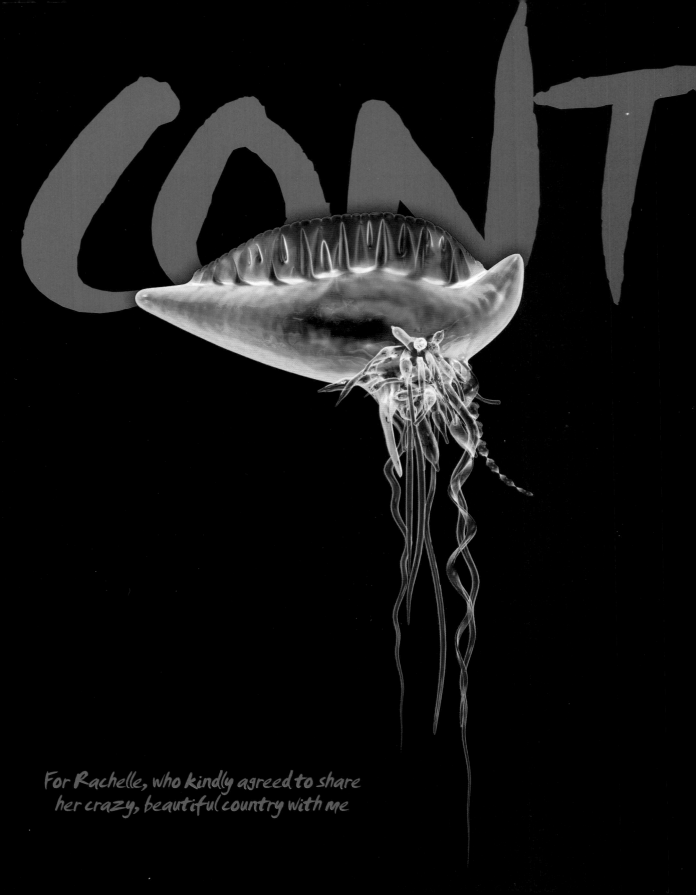

For Rachelle, who kindly agreed to share
her crazy, beautiful country with me

ON!

It's a place so nuts that there are no rules except the one rule to rule them all: if it's totally unlikely, almost certainly poisonous and definitely disgusting, it lives here.

Never leave your own house and you could still be nipped while having a shower, stung as you sit on the toilet, or bitten when you're floating in your pool.

Head outdoors for some fresh Aussie air and an army of nasties awaits, from a flightless bird with velociraptor moves to an angry ant who's not here to picnic. And that's only if the road itself doesn't kill you first.

Run to the water for a cool dip and take your chance among a fisherman's basket of predators with fangs, fins and freakishly deadly tentacles designed to make you suffer.

Then there's just the everyday Aussie crazy, like unbelievable weather and natural disasters.

Yep, there's a whole lot of weird out there. But we love it. Australians are known for their resilience and their ability to make light in the face of danger. And, because it's pretty much a dead cert that someone will always get just a little too close, we'll usually have a couple of happy snaps and a tale to tell about it.

So sit back (check for spiders first), relax (unless you're near the water) and enjoy these local legends.

CROC

Big, strong, tough as sh*t and ready for action. And that's just the ute carrying him.

Fortunately for both photographer and driver, the croc in this pic is dead – captured and shot at Palumpa, in the Northern Territory, after 'menacing the kids' for two years. Turns out the massive 4.5-metre saltie had been making it hard for local children to cross a causeway and get to school in the morning, so authorities had to, er, wade in. They loaded the beast into the tray with a backhoe, an act that serves to illustrate a freaky visual point – a croc as big as a pick-up?

6

There are so many crocs in Australia's tropical north that the nation's greatest newspaper, the *NT News*, once published a front page made up entirely of crocodile yarns. Between Broome and Gladstone, crocodiles are such a fact of life that no one bats an eyelid when they see one speeding past on the back of a ute.

In this country, 'A croc walks into a bar' is no joke but an uncomfortable reality. Crocs regularly stumble into watering holes (the sort that serve beer), block roads, park themselves in garages and take bites out of boats. They've stolen tradies' chainsaws, spent nights in prison cells and forced visiting US presidents to take out croc insurance. They're basically a wonderful menace to society.

So bound-up are crocs with Australia's self-identity that our highest-grossing movie at the local box office (*Crocodile Dundee*, $48m) and most famous conservationist (the late Steve 'The Crocodile Hunter' Irwin) are inexorably linked to the world's most successful reptile.

Yep, crocs are after blood. And possibly fame. And if some 'Croc Head' goes swimming in their pool, he's going to get munched. But why not? They were here first. Anyway, let these louche lizards speak for themselves.

Crocs are big.
Like f*cking
MASSIVE.

Look at this guy. He's the second-biggest crocodile ever caught in Australia and was snared by Matt Wright, well-known Territory chopper pilot, croc hunter and star of the National Geographic Channel's *Outback Wrangler*.

Weighing a whopping 890 kilograms and measuring 5.58 metres, this croc is bigger than reigning local champ Brutus. After a few big feeds, he may even supersede Cassius, a male saltie captured in the NT but now living on Green Island off Cairns who, at 968 kilograms and 5.48 metres, is currently the world's largest croc in captivity.

Why the Roman names? Is it a nod to Russell Crowe's *Gladiator*? Should we expect to see a Maximus emerge from the mud to claim the biggest croc bastard title? Or a Caesar? Certainly, the *NT News* could go to town. We can see it now: 'Hail, Caesar'!

#1

OZ FACT

Croc wrangling has been a fact of Top End life ever since the days of the much-feared Sweetheart, whose stuffed body now scares kids at Darwin's museum. Sweetheart was more than 5 metres long and weighed 780 kilograms when he was caught in 1979. He'd made a name for himself (not to mention a cheesy nickname) after a series of attacks on outboard motors, dinghies and fishing boats in NT waters over five years.

#2
Crocs are 'good' news.

The mighty *NT News* features crocodile tales on an almost daily basis, and it's easy to see why. 'Crocs sell,' explains former editor Matt Cunningham, a Victorian who enjoyed his stint risking death in Darwin so much he recently returned as Bureau Chief for Sky News. 'They live side by side with humans, and they CAN KILL YOU!'

And not just you. The muddy rivers of the Territory are theoretically the perfect environment for another Aussie nasty, the bull shark. But when one such big guy strayed 80 kilometres up the infamous 'croc-infested' Adelaide River he swam into the 'hood of Territorian legend Brutus, the river's most famous, most fearsome resident.

'We'd fed Brutus on the bank earlier and were coming back past and we saw something in his mouth,' lucky Sydney photographer Andrew Paice told the *NT News* after capturing the epic battle. 'The shark was still alive. Brutus took it back into the water and then started to shake it around a bit. He then went back into the mangroves like he was protecting his prey.'

The expression on the shark's face is pure horror. 'Oh shit, *that's* why my mum said never take the shortcut home ...'

Brutus, who's said to be around 80 years old, apparently lost his front leg in a shark attack. If the story's true then revenge is definitely a dish best served cold. With fins.

We love a nickname. David becomes Davo, Elizabeth turns into Liz and Warne will always be Warnie. And so it goes that the most terrifying of our predators, the saltwater crocodile, is fondly referred to as a 'saltie'. Ain't that cute?

There's a strict hierarchy when it comes to crocodiles, whether they're sharing their territory with more of the same species or with any other breathing thing that strays onto their patch. The oldest, meanest, baddest crocs are top of the food chain, and will demolish anything that gets in their way.

So, basically the hierarchy goes:
#1 = big f*cking saltie;
#2 = everything else (f*cked).

Pictured here is the dramatic – and typically WTF – moment a big saltie decided to show a visiting freshie who was boss. This is no fond frolic between long-lost cousins but a take-no-prisoners throwdown, which shows that for salties, at least, blood is not thicker than water.

How do you tell the difference between a saltie and a freshie? Well, freshies are smaller, often paler in colour, with thinner snouts and smaller teeth. But if you're ever in the position to compare, there are probably other things you need to think about. Like getting the f*ck out of there.

OZ FACT
Mad, bad and dangerous to know, salties have been accused of cannibalism, but they don't eat their young. Yes, crocodile mothers do carry their young in their mouths – but for protection, not for a quick snack. Relax, people.

Saltwater crocodiles take *zero* f*cking prisoners. #3

#4 Crocs can take to the *skies.*

Not content with owning their natural habitat – both rivers AND the ocean – salties are also highly dangerous on land. And just when you thought 'Okay, as long as they stay horizontal I can deal', they stick it to you by leaping right out of the goddamn water. Yes, really!

Where else but Australia would a thriving, competitive boat-tour market take tourists so up-close-and-personal that the wild 5.5-metre crocodile jumping for food beside your boat could eat out of your hand – or even eat your hand?

On the famous 'jumping crocodile cruises' (you can't say you weren't warned), the crocs on the NT's Adelaide River jump for pig snouts on the end of poles while wide-eyed tourists gawk. In fact, this replicates the crocs' natural behaviour when they're trying to snare brolgas, sea eagles, magpie geese and other passing birds.

Experienced guides have been working these waters since the early 1970s, and it's highly

OZ FACT
A huge 70 per cent of the food a crocodile eats is converted into flesh and energy (in humans, this applies to only 3 per cent of food consumed). So crocs can survive for months without eating.

recommended that visitors enjoy this wildlife attraction behind their boats' thick glass rather than venturing out on their own.

'Where's a safe spot to fish?' ponders Adelaide River Cruises owner Morgan Bowman. 'There are no safe spots. If you are a Territorian, you know not to go in the water.'

And if you're not a Territorian?

'Stay out of the water.'

But every now and then someone, somehow, manages to put themselves smack-bang in the habitat of the scariest f*cking creature on the planet.

So if that's you, what do you do? A crocodile's faster than you, stronger than you and can hold his breath much longer than you – plus he definitely has more teeth.

Well, if these lucky escapes are anything to go by, it's the eyes that have it.

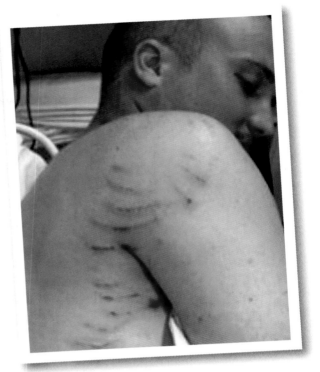

Darwin kitesurfer Chris Keeping (pictured here) got stranded 100 metres offshore in deep water when his kite became tangled. 'I didn't see him until the last minute, and then he smashed me like a Mack truck,' says Keeping of his croc encounter. Keeping eventually poked the crocodile in the eye until it dropped him from its jaws. He survived.

Father of three Eddie Sigai punched, kicked and gouged a crocodile that latched onto his hand as he swam with his daughters at a waterhole near Weipa in north Queensland, a place he'd swum all his life.

'All I can remember is grabbing it, shaking it, punching it and going for its eyes,' he says. He survived.

Noosa man Mick Curwen was night-snorkelling off Lizard Island in Far North Queensland to watch coral spawning when a crocodile grabbed him by the arm. He managed to shock the croc into releasing him by shining his dive torch into its eyes. He survived.

'I'll leave my night-time dips to the swimming pool,' Mick said with typical Aussie humour.

This guy is one of the *lucky* ones. #5

Who you gonna call?

Crocbusters!

New York can keep its Ghostbusters – we've got a much tougher team here. These guys are full-time Crocbusters, professional 'crocodile managers' (LOL) who risk way more than getting slimed every day.

The NT Parks and Wildlife Crocodile Management Team work in hot, dirty, dangerous conditions. They're the people you call when a crocodile is menacing your chooks. Or your dog. Or you. Key tools? Duct tape and cable ties. Just don't cross the beams!

They have their work cut out: there are estimated to be at least 100,000 wild crocs in the NT, and more people were killed by crocodiles in 2014 than in any year since records began. Saltwater crocs killed four Territorians in 2014: one-fifth of the total 21 people killed since 1974.

'We're trying to get the CrocWise message across as best as possible,' NT wildlife ranger Tom Nichols told AAP. 'Unfortunately we will get another [death], we just don't know when.' It's a problem when so many recreational activities enjoyed by Territorians and Far North Queenslanders, such as fishing, swimming, camping, boating and bushwalking, bring people and crocs close together, increasing the risk of an attack. How can you stay safe? 'Stay away from the water, don't put your hands near the water.' Could a message be any clearer?

Australia's most *famous* conservationist was 'The Crocodile Hunter'

It's a typical Australian irony that the man dubbed 'The Crocodile Hunter' was a passionate advocate for the beast's survival.

'Crocodiles are easy,' Steve Irwin once famously said. 'They try to kill you and eat you. People are harder. Sometimes they pretend to be your friend first.'

Only in Australia would the nation's most beloved entertainer be a man who took his one-month-old son, Bob, into a 3.8-metre-long crocodile enclosure during feeding time at Irwin's Australia Zoo. The incident stirred up international controversy and afterwards the Queensland's government changed the law to prohibit adults from taking kids into enclosures.

Yet still we couldn't get enough of the guy who made 'Crikey' cool.

At least Steve Irwin's American wife, Terri, knew what she was getting into – the couple spent their honeymoon filming segments for his hit TV series *The Crocodile Hunter*. At the peak of its popularity, the Animal Planet show was viewed by more than 500 million people in 200 countries, with Irwin eventually appearing in both *The Simpsons* and *South Park*. What a legend!

Steve Irwin died at 44 doing what he loved – flirting with danger around deadly animals. He was only the third person to be killed by a stingray in Australia. He will never be forgotten.

OZ FACT

After Irwin's death in 2006 a huge public memorial service, introduced by Russell Crowe, was held in Australia Zoo's Crocoseum. Broadcast live throughout Australia, the US and the UK, it was estimated to have been seen by more than 300 million viewers worldwide.

#7

#8 For every croc, there's a ~~croc-crazy~~ local.

Steve Irwin was exceptional, but he wasn't the exception. From Broome in Western Australia to Gladstone in Queensland, crocodiles are a fact of life. So many locals have decided that if you can't beat them you might as well join them.

Australia's tropics are inhabited by men (they're always men) who claim to have grown up with crocs or possess a unique ability to communicate with them. Occasionally these characters even have all their fingers.

One such (typically bearded) adventurer is 66-year-old Queenslander Rob Bredl, who claims it is nearly impossible to starve in the Australian wilderness if you can overcome your 'barrier of repulse'. Dubbed 'The Barefoot Bushman', Bredl claims to have been bitten more than 40 times by crocs yet still enjoys riding an 800-kilo monster – one of dozens he owns – on his 175-acre Blue Planet wildlife park.

'When it comes to crocs, everyone wants the drama, the danger,' Bredl once told the *Daily Mail*. 'I must be the luckiest, crazy person who has ever lived. I have been bitten by snakes and crocodiles and I'm still here.'

You heard him. Moral of the story? To live a long and prosperous life in Australia, you need to be a little bit insane. Okay, totally batshit.

OZ FACT

The hunting of Aussie crocodiles for their skins resulted in their near extinction. In 1970, the estuarine crocodile was officially protected from hunting. Since then, crocodile populations have increased – today, Australia is home to an estimated 100,000 crocs.

Despite all the warnings, one *lunatic* will always cross the line.

#9

And not just Australians, of course. These pictures show Israeli tourist Novon Mashiah running for his life as a crocodile lunges at him on Yellow Waters lake in the Territory.

Just a few frames – and seconds – separate the image of 27-year-old Mr Mashiah pointing out the swimming crocodile while posing for a photograph and the moment the 4-metre-long reptile 'suddenly exploded' out of the water.

The pics appeared in the good old *NT News*, that purveyor of classic croc stories, under the headline 'G'day Bait!'. Ah, Australia. We try to kill you – then we pun about it.

'I was shocked – the animal clearly wanted to kill me,' Mr Mashiah told the paper. 'One minute I was leaning over the boat teasing it for a picture. The next minute it burst out of the water with incredible speed ... its jaws fully open. I was shaking.'

Mr Mashiah wasn't the first and no doubt won't be the last. The story goes that one woman even tried planking on a (muzzled and tied-down) 4.65-metre croc during the height of the craze in 2011.

According to the awesomely named Chase Johnson, Crocodile Manager at Darwin's Crocosaurus Cove, it's common for crocs to attack boats. 'There is a theory among crocodile experts that motors have the same vibration and sound as male crocs in breeding season,' Johnson told the *NT News*.

Either way, waving your hand at crocs is not going to help you. Just. Leave. Them. Alone.

OZ FACT
Habitat destruction is now considered a major threat to crocodile survival in northern Australia. Increasingly, humans are crowding in on crocodile territory – developments in swamps, mangroves and rivers are displacing crocodiles from their homes.

SNAK

Snake fan? You're in the right place. Australia is ophiophilist nirvana ... home to some 140 species of slithering delights.

If, however, like most of us you're in the snakes-are-totally-bad Indiana Jones camp, then Terror Australis is a place to avoid. Always a nation to up the freak-out ante, the Land Down Under is known for its spectacularly dangerous snakes.

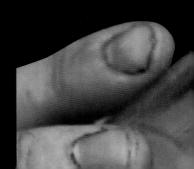

These serpentine show-offs have earned a fearsome global reputation, with 20 of the world's 25 most venomous snakes being Aussies.

Among this charming group is the Inland Taipan (pictured here kindly donating some venom), undisputed champion of the world if you're looking for a bite that leads to the worst headache of your life, severe nausea, violent vomiting, agonising abdominal pain, physical collapse (as in you really shouldn't be standing, mate) and rapid paralysis. Closely followed by death – though, according to experts at the Australian Museum, this guy (the so-called 'fierce snake') is actually a 'shy … relatively placid creature'. Course it is.

Amazingly, Australia has so many vicious snakes that one is known simply as the Common Death Adder – because, let's face it, there's nothing so common as a deadly snake, right? Don't panic, though: despite the fact that there are so many snakes just waiting to sink their fangs into you, the wide availability of antivenom today means only one or two Aussie dies from a snake bite each year on average – in contrast to India, where snakes cause more than 45,000 deaths per annum. If you're interested, the process of extracting venom from a snake is called 'milking' – almost sounds sweet, doesn't it?

Snakes will eat *anything*,

#10

even bats.

You're out for a nice, relaxing stroll in your quiet, safe street, sucking on your latte and admiring your retro Converse sneakers, when you round a corner and come straight upon a scene right out of a horror movie. The words 'Motherf*cking jeepers creepers!' come to mind – if you're not already screaming.

A lethally large carpet python has a very unfortunate flying fox locked in a deathly embrace. Yep, a flying fox – Australia's biggest bat – which, if not quite a giant demon, is certainly more than an appetiser, even for a 4-metre snake weighing up to 15 kilos.

Perhaps this dinner interrupted wouldn't be quite so shocking if it occurred out of sight

in the treetops, but this snack is taking place on a suburban street enjoyed by unsuspecting cats, dogs and toddlers. If a hungry snake can happily dine on a gigantic bat with a wingspan of more than a metre, what else can he eat, we ask?

Carpet pythons are not typically aggressive, according to those in the know, but we're not entirely reassured. 'Theoretically it could kill a very small child,' said one expert after a large python, seen still digesting its prey, freaked out a bunch of Queensland mountain bikers in early 2016.

He continued: 'Or even an adult if you let it wrap around your chest and neck and didn't fight back.'

Note to self: FIGHT BACK!

OZ FACT

Six-year-old Tyler Thurgood was attacked in his top-bunk bed (yes, top bunk) by a three-metre-long carpet python near Macksville, NSW, in February 2016. His mother, Tamara, was woken by her son's terrifying scream. 'It was like a nightmare,' she told the *Nambucca Guardian*. 'I didn't know what had happened, I certainly didn't think it involved a snake.' Even though the snake was wrapped around her son's stomach, Tamara managed to pull it off and little Tyler survived.

So you're out in the middle of nowhere, minding your own business in Western Australia's remote Pilbara region, when you spot a snake embarking on a colossal Happy Meal. Twenty-four hours later he's still digesting, and your photos have become a viral sensation.

Irish mining engineer Trevor McGowan and his mates watched, amazed, as this determined black-headed python consumed a sand goanna as big as itself over five hours at a minesite road on Fortescue Metals Group's Cloudbreak Mine.

Sand goannas are carnivorous monitor lizards that hunt snakes and are apparently immune to the venom of even the most dangerous, such as the Inland Taipan.

One particular goanna, though, clearly came a cropper, but if this book proves anything, it's that the only rule in the Outback is: THERE ARE NO RULES!

Snakes eat *lizards.*

#11

Snakes #12

One of the wonderful things about Australia's bevy of beastly critters is that you can never be sure who's going to beat who in a fight. One minute a crocodile's munching a shark; the next a crocodile's being eaten by a snake. Welcome to Oz, where your next meal could be your last.

In 2014 onlookers marvelled at a dramatic fight to the death between a water python and a freshwater croc at Lake Moondarra, Queensland.

'[The crocodile] was fighting at the start, so it was trying to keep its head out of water and survive,' Mount Isa mother Tiffany Corlis told ABC North West Queensland. 'But as the morning progressed, you could tell that both of them were getting a little weaker. Finally, the croc sort of gave in and the snake uncoiled for a little while, had a brief break and then actually started to consume the crocodile.'

Marvin Muller snapped this now-iconic picture of the final moments of the four-hour battle. 'Pretty cool experience, not something you think you're going to see but I guess up in Mount Isa you see some pretty cool things,' Muller told the ABC.

You sure do, mate.

OZ FACT When curiosity killed five cats, ambushed by scrub pythons in Cairns in January 2016, some cat owners were devastated. Others, though, were like, 'Oh well, we live in north Queensland. Shit happens.' Yes, it does.

eat crocodiles. 'Nuff said.

#13

In case you fall into a waterhole in WA's Kimberley region any time soon, it's good to know you'll be 'rescued'. This wallaroo took a wrong turn he almost certainly regretted, but for this beautiful – f*cking huge – olive python, it was a fishing trip to remember.

'Huge' may not be a strong enough word to describe this snake – look to the right of the photograph and you'll see his body goes right out of shot.

Taken in 2005, the image captures a creature that has been described by some as Australia's Schrödinger's cat. Did he eventually manage to take away his tantalising treat? Did he have the strength to haul a large 20-kilo macropod into his stomach? Or is he still there, trying to figure out how to go get the BBQ sauce?

Snakes can pick up their *own* takeaway.

OZ FACT

Australia's second biggest snake after the scrub python, olive pythons are often snapped lying immobilised after biting off more than they can chew. They can take 5 to 7 days to digest a big wallaby, after which they sleep it off for 4 to 8 weeks before looking for another meal.

You could call it the perfect laxative, because a sight like this would be enough to make you crap yourself.

Called in to help one north Queensland resident, Townsville snake catcher Elliot Budd had to unbolt the toilet to pull this 3-metre carpet python out of its watery haven. A week later he was summoned to another toilet, where he had to get his hand right down inside the pan to coax out a 2.5-metre snake whose body was almost entirely down the pipes.

Snakes can *sleep* in your toilet.

#14

'At first I thought it was a friend having a go at me but [the owner] was serious,' recalls Elliot.

Funny that in Australia, even the snake catcher's first instinct is to assume two loo lizards in a week must be a joke.

So why would a snake head for the throne room? Well, in Australia's tropical north, snakes grow fat as kings during the wet season, so at the end of the dry season or during a drought they slither off in search of water. And they're not fussy.

Yep, the tropical north is a VERY exciting places to live. Here, WC stands for Weird Crap, and even a visit to the can is an extreme sport.

#15 Snakes can *hang* in your shower.

Like soap-on-a-rope from hell, this is the horrific sight that greeted a group of Brisbane flatmates one evening. Deciding against showering with their 2.2-metre visitor, they called in snake catcher Bryan Robinson.

Bryan found the snake had forced its way in through a loose light fitting. 'Just the weight of the snake may have been enough to push the cover off,' he told Westside News.

Big snakes are everyday stuff for people living in Australia's tropical north, and they're a business opportunity for snake removalists across Queensland.

Among his career highlights, Cairns snake catcher Dave Walton recalls snaring a 5-metre, 18-kilogram female python that had

been enjoying an orgy with five male snakes in the roof of an outrigger canoe club in the appropriately named suburb of Yorkeys Knob. The frisky snake was finally captured with the help of National Geographic TV's *Python Hunters*. Walton also once found four snakes living in the roof of a Cairns home after residents reported 'loud thumping and thrashing noises'.

Port Douglas toddler Kye Dalton had a lucky escape on Boxing Day 2011, when an amethystine python bit him as he was playing in the family carport. Neighbours heard screams and came to the rescue, eventually subduing the snake.

Kye lost consciousness during the one-hour trip to Cairns Base Hospital but was discharged the next day with bite marks and bruising.

Two days later, as the 4-metre culprit was being removed from the roof, the plucky little Aussie legend waved and shouted, 'Bye, bye Bitey!'

OZ FACT
At least one in five homes in Queensland has a snake living in the roof. 'They thrive around suburbia,' says snake catcher Andrew Smedley. 'I'd like to encourage people to leave them because they're real good for vermin control. They'll clean out your rats, your possums – you name it.' Yeah, all right, mate.

It's Tuesday morning, you've just popped into your friendly neighbourhood op shop to browse worn copies of *Australian Geographic* **and old-man shirts when … 'WTF is that?!'**

A F*CKING MASSIVE SNAKE is what!

Thankfully, 65-year-old former snake breeder turned wrangler Virginia McGrath was nearby the day a 6-metre amethystine python popped into Ingham's St Vincent de Paul store.

OZ FACT

Virginia McGrath's teenage grandson Wyatt once saved his nanna's life after a 4-metre python handcuffed her wrists together with its coils. 'It was days before the imprint of my watch disappeared from where it had pressed into my skin,' she recalls. The legendary snake wrangler has had more than her fair share of close encounters with reptiles in her time. Once she kindly took a severely constipated 3.2-metre snake to the vet, who ended up removing a massive 2.7-metre load of shit from its body. 'He was all blocked up,' she explains. Poor lad.

'It was dangerous stuff,' Virginia told the *Courier Mail* after cornering the scrub snake underneath a second-hand clothes rack. 'He could kill me if he wanted to. They can get a couple of coils around you and you can't breathe.'

Australia: where even the most innocuous perusal of vintage clothing could suddenly become a life and death struggle with a killer snake. Fangs for the memories …

#16

Snakes enjoy a trip to the *shops.*

#17

Snakes like to *travel*.

From the nation who brought you the Flying Kangaroo, we now present Snakes on a Plane. For real. In 2013, cabin crew on Qantas flight QF191 from Cairns to Port Moresby in Papua New Guinea, no doubt expecting yet another request for peanuts, must have been ruffled when a traveller told them, 'There's a snake on the wing … there's its head and if you look closely you can see its body.'

Passengers were shocked to look out their cabin windows and see, not fluffy white clouds, but a 3-metre scrub python holding on for dear life.

Web designer Robert Weber, who shot a video of the snake that was soon being replayed around the world, told *the Sydney Morning Herald* that after the snake was initially tucked in quite neatly, the wind caught its tail and pulled it out, and the rest of the trip became 'a life and death struggle' for this infrequent flyer.

The plucky python somehow managed to hold on for the entire 1-hour, 50-minute

flight at a speed of 400 kilometres per hour and temperatures of minus 12°C. But the relentless wind smashed it against the side of the plane, splattering blood across the engine, and sadly, ground crew found the snake dead on arrival.

While perhaps not quite as dramatic as the Samuel L. Jackson original, featuring only one solo snake rather than a whole crate, this breaking-news story was a global smash and one of smh.com.au's most viewed stories of 2013, with more than a million page views.

OZ FACT

Qantas appeared to have a bit of a snake problem in 2013. A few months after the Port Moresby incident, 370 Tokyo-bound passengers spent the night in a Sydney hotel after a small Mandarin rat snake was discovered aboard QF21 shortly before take-off. While this type of snake doesn't pose any threat to humans (apart from that of pants-peeing fear), the airline (very sensibly) decided to postpone the flight and do a thorough search on the off-chance that the snake wasn't alone.

Some snakes get their own *police* escorts. #18

So you're on your way home from your mate's house when you come across two coppers spotlighting a log covering the entire width of the road. You slow down so as not to damage your tyres, only to discover that the 'log' is actually a large python that the nice policemen are trying to coax off the road.

Ah, Australia, land of jokers great and small. The Queensland Police Service has earned a global reputation for its entertaining, occasionally ridiculously cheesy social media updates, so it's probably unsurprising that they uploaded this incident to Facebook with the status: 'Snakes on a plain. This officer's dedication scaled new heights when dealing with this slippery character.' ROTFL. No wait, that's the snake.

OZ FACT

Basically, be careful on the roads, right? Cos you just never know when a snake is out there waiting for you. In 2015 a man walking all the way around Australia in Stormtrooper armour to raise funds for a Melbourne children's hospital was bitten on the shin by a king brown snake. Thankfully, the armour did its job which is just as well as we all know that Stormtroopers can't use the force.

SPIDE

Asking people to rank which species of Australian creature they're most afraid of is ridiculous: there are so many to choose from!

But for most of us suburb-dwellers, spiders are right up there. And the reason? They pop up frickin' EVERYWHERE. This is a nation, remember, that glories in a song called 'The Redback on the Toilet Seat', released in 1972 by country music singer Slim Newton (not to be confused with country legend Slim Dusty) and sadistically covered by several artists since.

Okay, the space invader pictured here may not be resting on the toilet seat (perhaps the python from the previous chapter scared him off), but he's close enough for extreme discomfort. Spiders, you see, are happy to get as near to you as they like. And sure, he's not a redback but rather a giant big f*ck off huntsman, a household constant in Australia about which we'll find out more in this delightful chapter.

That's another thing about spiders. We've got lots! Hairy? Tick. Large? Yup. Fast and scuttly? You bet. You want deadly with that? Well, Australia just happens to boast the world's most venomous species – the eponymous Sydney funnel web, meanest bastard of all. Like, make you drop down dead bad. Although such is our nation's spirit of fair competition that Melbourne is fast playing catch-up with an unwelcome boom in redback spider bites. Is this the moment where we point out that, thanks to anti-venom, there have actually been zero spider-related fatalities since 1979? No, really!

#19 Spiders have *zero* concept of personal space.

Your toilet paper, your showerhead, you name it. These guys are fond of a domestic scene, so much so that most Australians are familiar with the spine-tingling feeling of having a huntsman perve at them from some corner of the room. EVERYWHERE, remember?

Yet despite being able to rival *Psycho* for shower-scene horror, the huntsman is technically a non-aggressive spider. It will usually try to run away rather than take you on, and can even help control your cockroach situation, according to experts. And it moves FAST. Huntsmen are termed 'social spiders', which means they display 'cooperation among mutually tolerant individuals'. They're basically just like us, working together to hunt prey and care for their young. Yeah, nah!

Buuut (and there's always a but), huntsmen do possess venom and can give a pretty painful bite – which you definitely shouldn't look up on Google Images. So remember that the next time you're going for a shower and find a 'harmless' huntsman staring down at you with its eight eyes. Yes, it's large and hairy, but so is – well, best not to Google that either.

OZ FACT

Recently, a huge huntsman was found (and filmed) crawling around inside a Woolworths supermarket salad bag, which if nothing else proves a) that Woolies' salads are free from chemical sprays and b) that spiders love Italian Style Salad. Unsurprisingly, Woolies' Facebook page was inundated with smart-arse comments. 'I hope they set the bag of salad on fire,' said one contributor. 'This is why you don't make friends with salad,' joked another. Shudder!

Spiders make *fools* of our menfolk.

If you're an Australian male, or aspiring to that lofty title, you'd better be damn sure you've perfected your spider-capturing technique.

The bloke in this picture appears to be in control of the situation, thanks to his trusty Tupperware container and keen focus ... but appearances can be deceiving. The picture is from a clip, filmed by his young daughter, that has had more than 29 million views on YouTube since it was posted.

'I decided to get a bigger container because of the size of this one,' Dad narrates confidently. 'I'll have to move really quick.'

Cue the chaos. Man misses spider. Spider drops to floor and scuttles away. Man stumbles down ladder and gets caught in container. Daughter screams and drops camera, her last words replaying for eternity: 'I told you not to play with spiders.'

The internet is overflowing with hilarious out-takes of Aussie men trying to prove

their manhood. Specimen one (Failure) is wearing a motorbike helmet, R.M.Williams boots and gardening gloves and still makes an absolute hash of it. Specimen two (Alpha Aussie Bloke) is wearing a Chesty Bonds singlet and pluggers and can remove spiders in his sleep.

Huntsman spiders: the only harmless things that make grown men scream with terror. So impressive, in fact, were one man's screams that police were called to a Sydney unit by worried neighbours who suspected domestic violence. They reported sounds of a woman hysterically screaming and a man's voice shouting, 'I'm going to kill you, you're dead!'

The police transcript on their Facebook page is arachno-gold:

Male: 'It was a spider, a really big one!'

Police: 'What about the woman screaming?'

Male: 'Yeah, sorry, that was me. I really, really hate spiders.'

#21

You know that phrase 'Objects in mirror are closer than they appear'? Well, that just sucks.

While few people die from spider attacks in Australia, the huntsman (harmless huntsman, remember him?) and his mates still manage to cause a fairly sizable annual death toll thanks to their annoying tendency to hide in the sun visors, dashboards and mirrors of cars, freaking out drivers so much they cause accidents.

Most Australian motorcyclists have had at least one 'huntsman inside visor' scenario, which explains why they tend to check their helmets before pulling them on. On school runs every day across Australia, mothers deal with huntsmen lurking on headrests and child seats – you try flicking a spider out of the window while negotiating 20 roundabouts.

When Patrick Futcher posted this picture of a huntsman mother with a brood of babies on his wing side mirror to social network Reddit, members of the community told him to be brave and prepare for some unwanted visitors inside his car soon. And, sure enough, in no time he was snapping an all-grown-up baby INSIDE his speedo dashboard. Which just proves you can escape your friends but you can't escape family.

Spiders like to hang in your *car*.

Spiders like to hang by your *pool.*

You've probably heard that Australia's oceans are full of unimaginable horrors – which is why many houses have a backyard pool. Why risk death when all you want is a refreshing dip?

Unfortunately, no one told Mother Nature – it turns out that suburban swimming pools and their surroundings are basically just motherf*cking death traps.

How so? The backyards of Australia are crawling with 43 species of funnel-web spiders, including six particularly dangerous, highly toxic and venomous types whose fangs are large, powerful and capable of penetrating soft shoes. Who even wears soft shoes in this country?

Perhaps for the same reasons as humans (a desire to chill out), or perhaps for another reason (an evil, spidery desire to kill), moisture-loving funnel-webs are attracted to water and consequently are often found around pool edges.

How big are these guys? In early 2016, the venom-milking program at the Australian Reptile Park received a 10-centimetre-wide male funnel-web dubbed 'Big Boy'. TEN CENTIMETRES WIDE! Think about it.

#22

35

Spiders like to hang

#23

N your f*cking pool!

Okay, so funnel-webs are all over your backyard, taking in the sun, enjoying the breeze. But surely you're safe underwater? Ah, nope.

Funnel-webs have their own scuba gear – their hairy abdomen traps oxygen bubbles when they fall into your pool. And just to really f*ck you up, even though they sink, they can survive for up to three days underwater – so never assume that a spider at the bottom of your pool is dead. Slowly, as their bodies get waterlogged, they lose the ability to stay buoyant and gradually sink and drown. You're crying now, right?

According to former spider keeper at Sydney's Taronga Zoo Joe Haddock, funnel-webs 'have lungs on the outside of their bodies, which are prone to drying out if it's not humid', making backyard pools the perfect place to rehydrate.

The list of symptoms triggered by a funnel-web bite are too scarily numerous to name here, but let's just say that in Australia, you'd be wise to check your shoes, your laundry, your pool, your pool's filter, your basically every bloody thing rather than risk a bite from any of Big Boy's kin. We're talking visible fang marks, here! And to make things worse, sometimes the spider will remain attached until you SHAKE IT OFF.

Funnel-webs even scare other funnel-webs. During mating, the male has to hold the aggressive female back with a spare pair of legs, then get the hell out of there after the deed is done to avoid being eaten.

Funnel-webs – terrorising a pool near you.

Spiders like camping. #24

Okay, Australia. Girt by sea and also, it seems, by countless spiders waiting to bite you, jump on you or just merrily scamper over you. Given that there's literally zero escape from our ever-ready arachnids, surely most sensible Australians would never leave the safety of their spider-free panic room?

Well, not quite … For as yet unfathomable reasons, some crazy folks actually get off on spending the weekend in Australia's great outdoors, pitching a tent and spending a couple of days trying to avoid getting killed by the local wildlife.

If you're camping, you'll definitely want to take a torch and a bucket and spend several hours scouring the field you've foolishly decided to share with hundreds of funnel-webs. At least this way, you might slightly lower your chances of needing a dose of antivenom before morning.

If you're lucky (or unlucky, depending on how you see it), you'll find a bunch of funnelwebs hanging out together, like these darling little babies. But where's Mum?

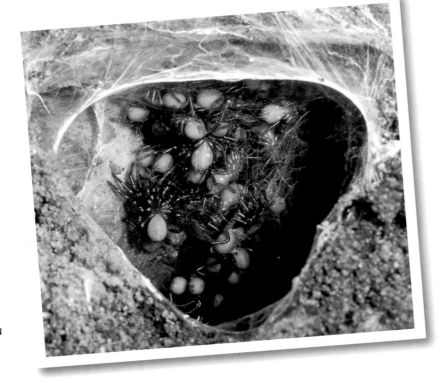

As if it wasn't enough that spiders are found *under* every single thing in Australia, they've also been spotted descending from the f*cking heavens. Welcome to Straya, where even the blue sky is full of terrors.

Not for the first time, spiders (yep, plural) were recorded parachuting in May 2015. 'A blanket of millions of baby spiders has been spotted falling from the sky,' reported the *Goulburn Post*. Apparently, at certain times of the year, young spiders keen to see the world will cast threads of webs and use them as parachutes to escape the ground and travel thousands of kilometres. WTF?!

'The whole place was covered in these little black spiderlings, and when I looked up at the sun it was like this tunnel of webs going up for a couple of hundred metres into the sky,' amazed Goulburn resident Ian Watson told *the Sydney Morning Herald*. 'You couldn't go out without getting spider webs on you. And I've got a beard as well, so they kept getting in that.'

Isn't nature fascinating? And no Aussie yarn is complete without a beard somewhere.

#25

Some days spiders just *rain* from the sky!

OZ FACT
Another spidery phenomenon with a similarly freaky outcome happens after floods, when tens of thousands of ground-based spiders weave webs to escape waterlogged ground.

No, this is not a scene from a 1960s Japanese sci-fi movie. This is just another day in the life of that little Aussie battler the redback spider.

Closely related to North America's black widow, the carnivorous, venomous redback is definitely our most impressive arachnid. Although insects are its usual prey, redback spiders have been spotted capturing much larger animals, as you can see in this charming action shot. And when you've taken on one lizard, what's to stop you facing off against snakes? That's right: redbacks have even been photographed snaring deadly eastern browns. Ballsy!

Female redbacks are the dangerous ones, and can grow up to 15 millimetres long: tiny but deadly, right?! These spiders are commonly found in sheltered spots such as under roof eaves and floorboards and in garden sheds, and their web is a tangle of dry silk with trailing trap lines designed to catch unsuspecting prey.

According to Aussie legend, redbacks are impervious to every known insect killer on the market. 'If it is resisting the aerosol spray, ignite the spray and burn the motherf*cker down!' recommends one commenter on Reddit. 'The spider, the house, the whole damn block even.'

Yeah, all right, mate, steady on.

Aussie spiders aren't afraid of *anything.* #26

OZ FACT
Redback spider bites are frequent occurrences, particularly through the Australian summer. More than 250 people receive doses of antivenom every year.

If even *birds* aren't safe, what chance have we got?

Perhaps the greatest story among Australia's arachno-files features Far North Queensland's golden orb spider, which, not content with his normal fare, decide to supersize his meal one afternoon in October 2008.

His choice? A chestnut-breasted mannikin, a type of finch, which became trapped in the spider's web in a backyard near Cairns. Given the golden orb, which is known for building strong webs, grows up to 50 millimetres in size and the bird more than double that, this was clearly the best day of this particular spider's life.

'It was an awful thing,' amateur photographer and bird enthusiast Les Martin told *The Cairns Post*. 'The spider was just chewing into its head … going up and down, and it was gouging into him at the top of his

beak. It was still wrapping it up.'

This story generated more than one million page views in 24 hours, the biggest the newspaper's website has ever seen, even bigger than the day Steve Irwin died.

Joel Shakespeare, head spider keeper at NSW's Australian Reptile Park (now there's a job), told the *Courier Mail*: 'Normally [golden orb spiders] prey on large insects, it's very unusual to see one eating a bird.'

Well, that's okay then.

OZ FACT
In 2012 an episode of the kids' TV show *Peppa Pig* was deemed unsuitable for broadcast in Australia because it said spiders were not really that scary. Not that scary? What a porkie!

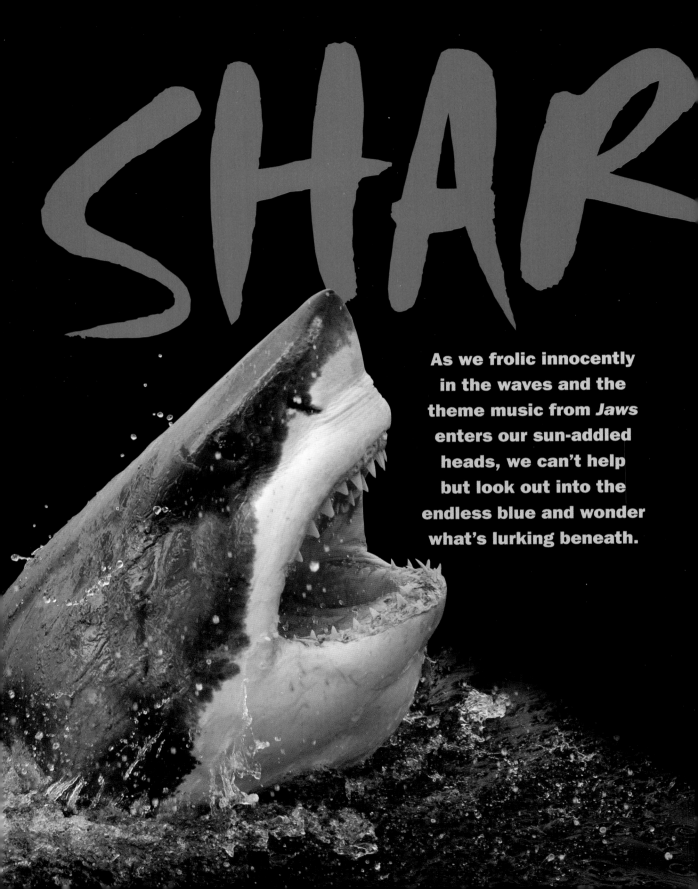

SHAR

As we frolic innocently in the waves and the theme music from *Jaws* enters our sun-addled heads, we can't help but look out into the endless blue and wonder what's lurking beneath.

There's something endlessly appealing/ horrifying about shark stories in Australia.

Every few months a photograph of a gigantic shark appears in local newspapers. And yes, NEWSFLASH, Australia is home to the great white, the tiger and the bull shark – the so-called 'Big Three'. These finned fiends are a) f*cking big fish, b) equipped with teeth designed to rip you apart, and c) often found swimming just off your favourite beaches. If crocs didn't convince you to Stay Out Of The Water, these bad boys will.

Actually, though, shark attacks are very rare. Australia is a nation of 24 million people, with more than 11,000 beaches to choose from and, since records began in 1791, there have been just 1025 shark attacks. Of these attacks, 234 have been fatal, according to the amazingly detailed Australian Shark Attack File kept by the Taronga Conservation Society. This means that in 225 years there has been on average one shark-related fatality per year. Compared with that, in 2015 alone, 271 people drowned in Australian waters, yet we're much more afraid of sharks than of rips.

What is it about these guys? They're among Earth's oldest life-forms and look just as creepy and prehistoric as we imagine they must have when they appeared more than 400 million years ago. They loom large in our imaginations because of the (pretty accurate) belief that being eaten by one would be a shitty, horrible way to die. And still, we can't get enough of them. We read every story going about them, we have a football team named after them, and one of our greatest golfers is nicknamed 'The Great White Shark'. (Don't even start us about the merchandise.) Sure, you can avoid the water but you can't avoid the hype …

Aussie sharks are very, very *very* LARGE.

#28

'It was that big!' is the catch-cry of fishermen everywhere. And when it comes to shark-spotting, it seems, size still matters.

When a 7-metre great white shark was reported just 100 metres off the coast of Adelaide, South Australia, in March 2016, swimmers were very sensibly evacuated from the scene. A debate ensued, with some calling it a 'fisherman's tale' and others vowing never to enter the water again.

Debate aside, as one punter posted, 'Don't really matter if it's 4-5-6 or 7 metres. It's a BIG shark! When your [sic] in the water with a White, what's a small one?' Spelling aside,

it's a good point, especially when you learn that Australia's waters are home to two of the world's largest populations of great whites, the apex marine predator.

In 2014, a couple of staff from Fisheries WA spent two and a half hours subduing a 1.6-tonne, 5.3-metre-long great white before fitting it with an internal tag – the biggest shark ever fitted with such a device. In case you're wondering, a Toyota HiLux, another popular, yet slightly less frightening, Aussie icon, is 4 metres long.

We're a nation that enjoys comparisons ('Call that a knife?' – remember?). And statistics. Here are two to ponder.

1) The odds of being attacked by a shark during your visit to the beach are less than 60 million to one.

2) Great white attacks on humans have increased by 50 per cent over the last decade.

Which fun fact are *you* gonna recall?

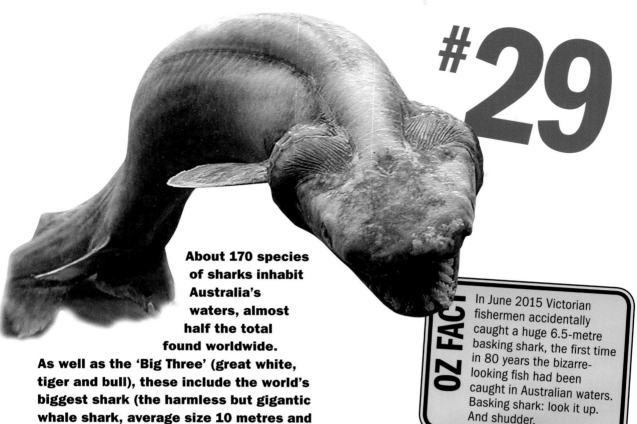

About 170 species of sharks inhabit Australia's waters, almost half the total found worldwide. As well as the 'Big Three' (great white, tiger and bull), these include the world's biggest shark (the harmless but gigantic whale shark, average size 10 metres and best spotted off Ningaloo Reef in WA) and the smallest (the 22-centimetre-long pygmy shark, best spotted in ... well, good luck with that).

But we also claim the ugliest. Of all the sharks that horrify Australians, by far the weirdest is the terrifying-looking creature fishermen hauled from the depths off Lakes Entrance, Victoria, in 2015. This Ridley Scott pin-up is the frilled shark, a 'living fossil' with 300 needle-shaped teeth in 25 rows (count them!) whose ancestry dates back 80 million years.

OZ FACT
In June 2015 Victorian fishermen accidentally caught a huge 6.5-metre basking shark, the first time in 80 years the bizarre-looking fish had been caught in Australian waters. Basking shark: look it up. And shudder.

'It is a freaky thing,' Simon Boag, from the South East Trawl Fishing Association, told the ABC. 'I don't think you would want to show it to little children before they went to bed.'

David Guillot, captain of the vessel that caught the shark, said he'd never seen anything like it in 30 years at sea. 'It was like a large eel, probably 1.5 metres long, and the body was quite different to any other shark I'd ever seen.'

Aussie sharks are f*cking *weird*.

Aussie sharks make good water *hazards*.

Sitting beside Queensland's Logan River, just south of Brisbane, Carbrook Golf Club may not quite rank with St Andrews or Augusta National for the quality of its fairways. But it's become famous for its own world-first feature: the bull sharks that have made the course's man-made lakes their home. Yep, only in Australia, right?

After juvenile sharks were swept across the golf course during a flood in 1995, fins started to be spotted five years later in the course's main lake – though initially sightings were jokingly dismissed as 'Queensland's Loch Ness Monster'. It wasn't until the club's general manager, Scott Wagstaff, captured footage and posted it on YouTube in 2011 that Carbrook became a global sensation.

This is definitely one course where you won't be taking off your shoes if your ball goes in the lake. Or indeed retrieving that ball, like, ever.

Perhaps embarking on their own Masters tour, bull sharks seem to be extending their territory in south-east Queensland as the human population grows: swimming in Gold Coast canals dramatically fell after two people were killed by bull sharks at Burleigh and Miami Lakes in the early 2000s.

OZ FACT

Bull sharks are one of the few shark species that tolerate freshwater for long periods, and have been reported in the Amazon, nearly 4000 kilometres from the sea. One of the most aggressive species of sharks with which humans regularly share water, the bull shark is the reason there are shark nets in Sydney Harbour.

Aussie sharks take *no* prisoners. #31

Steven Spielberg movie reels aside, sharks aren't deliberate maneaters. So why does an image of a 3.5-metre tiger shark circling a dolphin it's taken a chunk out of make us feel, well, a tiny bit anxious?

Pictures like this one, taken just off Burwood Beach in Newcastle in January 2015, send shivers down the spine of anyone who likes to spend the happy, lazy weeks between Christmas and Australia Day chilling out in the ocean. Which is basically everyone.

A massive 5-metre great white shark, spotted just 50 metres offshore, had already closed the city's beaches for a week when this bad boy rocked up and started hoeing into dolphins. Everyone loves dolphins – they're friendly, they're intelligent, they're sociable. Um, they're a bit like us.

Is that why we freaked out when we saw this pic? Were we worried that the shark was just making its way through the sushi buffet before turning to the main meal?

Dr Daniel Bucher, marine biologist at Southern Cross University, told the *Daily Telegraph*, 'If a shark is hanging around one particular area, it is a possibility that once it finds it can eat people it might shift its habits to take on a new reliable food source.' But he emphasises that this is a 'rare event'.

Here's hoping that's the only thing served rare in this scenario.

Shark-attack survivors have some *epic* scars. #32

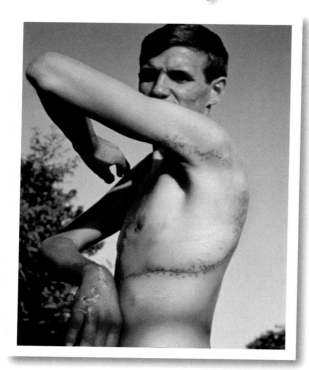

Rodney Fox has balls of steel. In 1963 the then 23-year-old survived a great white shark attack that left him with massive injuries and necessitated 462 stitches in his chest and 92 in his right hand and arm.

A former spear-fishing champion, when his physical (and psychological) wounds had healed he headed back into the water and embarked on a lifelong mission to discover as much as he could about the creature that almost killed him.

Inspired by a visit to Adelaide Zoo, where he saw the lions in cages, Fox decided to invert the invention and built the world's first 'shark cage' (to contain humans), in order to observe great whites safely underwater. He also set up the eponymous Rodney Fox Shark Expeditions which, 40 years on, still takes divers to South Australia's Neptune Islands to observe what Fox describes as Australia's 'keystone predator'.

That very first expedition into the great unknown was filmed by Fox's good mates and famous shark-fanciers Ron and Valerie Taylor. Their film, *Attacked By a Killer Shark*, is an Australian masterpiece that shows great whites not as 'crazy maneaters, but fascinatingly cautious creatures'.

'Yes, we have shark attacks here,' Valerie Taylor told *The Australian* in 2015. 'But I don't know one person who has survived a shark attack who blames the shark. It doesn't come up on the beach or up a street and grab you. You are a monster in its world. You made the decision to go into the water, and you have to live with it.'

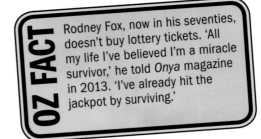

OZ FACT Rodney Fox, now in his seventies, doesn't buy lottery tickets. 'All my life I've believed I'm a miracle survivor,' he told *Onya* magazine in 2013. 'I've already hit the jackpot by surviving.'

Some people's beachside happy snaps are all about cocktails and sun-kissed smiles. But for Max Muggeridge, a shot ain't a shot without a shark in the foreground.

This keen angler became a global smash in 2015 after pics emerged of him posing with an impressive array of catches landed straight from the beach. In one month, Muggeridge caught a 3.8-metre tiger shark, a 3.7-metre hammerhead and a 2.7-metre bull shark. After tagging and photographing them with his girlfriend's assistance, the lifeguard from Queensland's Gold Coast threw them back.

In the course of a year, Muggeridge caught more than 200 sharks, with some catches taking longer than three hours to reel in – 'the kind of fight that brings you to your knees and crushes you mentally,' he reported.

Responding to suggestions that what he does is cruel, Muggeridge explained his method: 'I use special non-barbed circular hooks that stick in the corner of the jaw and slip out in less than five seconds. Then it's a quick tag, a quick photo and they're back in the water within 60 seconds.'

#33 Aussies catch *massive* sharks then throw 'em back!

In February 2014, the conservation group Sea Shepherd released a photo showing a male tiger shark hanging from a fishing boat off Moses Rock on the WA coast. The shark had fallen victim to WA's shark cull policy, formulated in response to seven fatal shark attacks in the south-west over three years.

A year later, there were calls for a cull of sharks off the NSW coast. Many applauded the idea. But others felt the ocean's delicate balance would be negatively affected. 'These sharks are protectors ... doing what they have done for as long as the oceans have existed,' commented Brooke Francisco on Facebook.

Surfer and conservationist Karl Goodsell claims that recent culls have had no impact on shark–human interactions.

'These high incidences of attacks are freak occurrences,' he says. 'The reality is that we need apex predators to ensure a healthy ecosystem balance in the oceans.'

Australian fisheries land hundreds of thousands of sharks per annum: an average of 8390 tonnes every year over the past five years, or about 4000 Toyota HiLuxes a year.

Globally, 1.4 million tonnes are killed each year – some 100 million sharks.

OZ FACT Either way, sharks are in a helluva pickle, with the Australian Marine Conservation Society estimating that 73 million sharks a year are killed for their fins. A single shark fin in Sydney's Chinatown costs $1000.

Aussie sharks #34 have more to fear from us than we do from them.

There's always someone who wants a *selfie* with a shark. # 35

We spend so much of our play time in and around their territory, and yet we're surprised when they attack us.

'As Australia's population continues to increase and interest in aquatic recreation rises, it would realistically be expected that there will be an increase in the number of shark encounters,' says Taronga Zoo's Shark Attack File.

Or, as Christopher Neff, a world expert at the University of Sydney, puts it bluntly, 'We're not prey, we're in the way.'

In most cases, sharks attack us when they mistake us for their usual prey (like confusing surfers with seals) or can't see where the f*ck they're going (like bull sharks in murky rivers).

What's more, most attacks are aborted after a single bite because the shark is a juvenile with jaws too weak to kill the victim.

Still, you'd be crazy to go that extra step and provoke them, wouldn't you? Except there's always someone willing to jump the shark …

And then there's the fake shark selfie, perfected in 2015 by teenager Alex Hayes. The shot of Alex sitting on his surfboard while a shark swam behind him enjoyed great success on Instagram and had UK paper *The Independent* convinced.

'I thought it was obvious from the start,' says Alex. 'It's their ocean, and if you're going to get eaten you're going to get eaten.'

OZ FACT
Interestingly, that same *Independent* reported last year (sore losers?) that 'more people have died while trying to take a selfie than from shark attacks'.

OTHER B

Crocs! Funnelwebs! Taipans! Great whites!

EASTIES

Okay, so Australia is home to a large percentage of the world's deadliest creatures. And yet alongside these threats to our sanity have evolved a collection of cuddly-looking animals who are not out to get us. Koalas, quokkas, quolls: Instagram thanks you.

Between these two ends of the spectrum lie some weird and wacky fauna that come into the 'only in Austraya' category. Birds that laugh at you. Birds that can't fly but would happily grind you to a pulp. Animals that lay eggs like birds and have bills like birds but, um, aren't birds. And then just freaky shit, great and small …

Take Chris. Poor bloke had been wearing about six years' worth of wool when RSPCA officers tracked him down in September 2015, following reports of a giant sheep roaming the ACT/NSW border. Among the batshit craziness of this story is the fact that Australia is so vast, a sheep can wander for that long without being bailed up.

Sedated so he wouldn't die from shock after such a long time without being sheared –

yes, seriously – Chris was left in the capable hands of Australian Shearing Championship winner Ian Elkins and four of his mates, who sorted out the wool-gatherer in a marathon 42-minute session.

Chris yielded a world-record 41.1 kilograms of fleece, ramming the previous title-holder, Big Ben – a New Zealand contender who contributed 28.9 kilos – into the shadows.

Aussies always tease their New Zealand neighbours about their fondness for sheep, but we're home to more sheep than any other nation, with a flock of more than 71 million. Not that we want to keep focusing on the competition between Australia and New Zealand in all things, but it is interesting to note that Chris's fleece could have produced about 205 Wallabies scarfs. Just sayin'.

#36 Some kangaroos can *smash* buckets with their bare hands.

Roger is ripped. Roger is built. But Roger isn't working out at Fitness First or busy training contestants on *The Biggest Loser*. Roger is a red kangaroo, the largest of his breed. Yep, cousin to those cuties we all photograph hippity-hopping about at zoos and wildlife parks.

This photo shows why you should never mess with a fully grown male red kangaroo. At nine years of age, dead-set legend Roger, who stands at 2 metres tall and weighs in at 89 kilos, boasts similar muscles to those of a bodybuilder, with defined biceps and triceps. That's because alpha males like Rog need to be expert kickboxers and wrestlers in order to fight off rivals intent on stealing their harem.

A kick from a big red kangaroo could disembowel you. 'A few unfortunate men have lost their tackle,' admits Roger's foster parent Chris 'Brolga' Barns, who reared the orphan joey by hand at his Kangaroo Sanctuary near Alice Springs, after Roger's mother was found dead on a highway.

'[He] will attack anyone or anything that gets too close to him and his women.'

OZ FACT

Male red kangaroos are renowned for crushing dogs trying to kill them. And not just dogs. In 2009 a Victorian farmer was attacked by 'a savage kangaroo' after he dived into a dam to save his blue heeler, Rocky – which the roo was trying to drown. Chris Rickard suffered gashes and cuts to his forehead, chest and abdomen. 'I don't think I'll ever be able to watch Skippy quite the same way,' he told the *Herald Sun*. 'It might bring back bad memories.'

Australia is home to some pretty goddamn crazy shit, but the unique species *Ornithorhynchus anatinus* takes the biscuit. It's almost like the punchline of one of those 'What do you get when you cross a …' jokes, yet it's totally for real.

An egg-laying mammal known as a monotreme, the platypus is such an eyeful, with its short fur and duck-like bill, that the first specimens to reach Europe in the 18th century were dismissed as elaborate hoaxes. (Like we'd bother!) But there's nothing fake about these freaking adorable beauties, as you'll discover if you mess with one.

Beneath the wonderfully WTF exterior, each of those dinky ankles on a male platypus features a sharp 15-millimetre-long spur attached to a venom gland in the leg.

One kick from this guy can kill a small dog or cause excruciating agony in humans that develops into hyperalgesia – increased sensitivity to pain – persisting for months.

Not only are platypus real, they're *venomous*.

#37

#38 Australia

is home to the original Angry bird.

For most Aussies, being attacked by a magpie is almost a rite of passage. These guys love to have a go at unprotected flesh, particularly during nesting season when they're guarding their young. So dangerous are they that people drive to the shops rather than risk their wrath, hide inside until they're gone, or wear cycle helmets (although they don't cycle) for protection. Oh, and did you know magpies recognise faces and can target the same folk every day?

A national survey found that 90 per cent of Aussie males and 72 per cent of women have been swooped upon at least once. The Injury Surveillance Information System that records hospital emergency department admissions revealed that in 59 magpie attacks over eight years, the eye was the birds' favoured target. The ISIS data (yep, ISIS) also found that cyclists were those most often attacked. So men on bikes are basically cruising for a serious bruising.

What to do? According to Darryl Jones, behavioural ecologist at Griffith University, you need to make yourself look 'completely ridiculous'. Options include sticking 'a forest' of cable ties out of your bike helmet so it looks 'like an echidna', or attaching a steel nut to a piece of string and whirling it like crazy above your head – though this might be particularly tricky/f*cking stupid if you are also trying to cycle at speed. Still feel in danger?

'The other thing that works really well is ugly rubber masks of witches and goblins,' Jones says. 'Worn backwards,' he adds.

Great, so not only can they recognise and attack us, they can also mock us. 'Here comes that idiot in the goblin mask again – yours or mine?'

57

In the Land Down Under you'll never need an alarm clock because the manic cackle of the kookaburra could wake the dead. In fact, one of the bird's nicknames is 'Bushman's Clock'. But while the king of the bush has inspired one of the nation's favourite nursery rhymes, it's not all sweetness and light. A perennially hungry carnivore, he's always looking to scoop up treats from barbecues, picnic tables, lunchboxes – even people's mouths. Watch the skies!

Kookaburras have a reputation for attacking their own reflection in windows, particularly in breeding season when they think they see a rival. Some birds have been known to accidentally stun or even kill themselves this way, which is no laughing matter.

Aboriginal tribes across Australia believed that the kookaburra's dawn chorus was a signal to the sky gods to light the great fire that illuminates the sky and warms the Earth.

It might feel like we're the butt of the kookaburra's joke when he flies off with our sangas, but he may be laughing at something else entirely. Kookaburras have a different laugh for just about every occasion, whether it's to warn off a rival or do a family roll-call.

OZ FACT

Larrikin Music, which holds the rights to 'Kookaburra Sits In the Old Gum Tree', successfully sued Aussie band Men at Work for copyright infringement, after alleging that part of the flute riff from the band's 1981 single 'Down Under' was copied from Marion Sinclair's 1932 nursery rhyme and song.

#39

Birds laugh at you as they *steal* your food.

People and cassowaries *don't* mix. #40

It's a confusing sign, this one, because despite the words, the car seems to be copping more damage than the cassowary. Two sides to every story, eh?

Demonised as Australia's most dangerous prehistoric-vintage bird, cassowaries are the 21st-century's answer to the velociraptor, with huge, dagger-like claws quite capable of gutting you. So when it comes to this big bird, first rule of thumb is to avoid it, especially the male when he's guarding his young. Standing as tall as a person, he'll stop at nothing to protect his brood – 71 per cent of cassowary victims have been chased, charged or karate-kicked by a pissed-off bird. Show some respect and you'll be right. Maybe. Hopefully.

The only documented human death caused by a cassowary occurred in 1926, when two teenage boys attacked a bird and it fought back big-time, killing one of them.

But as always, man poses a far greater threat to these beautiful birds than they do to us. Cassies are listed as endangered by Queensland's Department of Environment and

Heritage Protection, with only 1200 said to be left in the wild, living in the state's Wet Tropics and Cape York regions. Road deaths and unrestrained dogs are major causes of cassowary deaths here.

Whether you're in a car or crazy-ass-insane on foot, you should keep your eyes open when giant, freaky bird-spotting way up north. As those punsters at the Department of EHP put it: 'Be Cass-o-wary!!'

SPEEDING HAS KILLED CASSOWARIES

59

Yep, we have giant killer #41 centipedes.

In the harsh light of day it tucks itself away, chilling out under logs or leaf litter. But bring on night-time and this over-sized, over-limbed creepy-crawly comes out to hunt. What's more, it's well equipped for the task. Being an Australian beastie, of course this guy wields not one nasty weapon but two – large pincers and potent venom – giving him tools powerful enough to kill not just insects but small mammals, lizards, even snakes. The venom will hurt you too if you're brave/stupid enough to touch one of these nasties.

So what's it like running into a venomous centipede? 'I got up during the night to settle my son after a bad dream,' recounts Redditor Damon Adams. 'Then I went into the kitchen to grab a glass of water. I felt something touch the side of my foot like being lightly scratched with a fork. I quickly stepped back, turned on the light, and saw the beast scurrying towards me. I let out a noise I thought I had been incapable of since puberty and took a leap backwards.'

Just what do we mean when we say 'giant'? Well, these centipedes grow to about 16 centimetres – the length of three Freddo frogs but nowhere near as sweet. According to the Australian Museum website, humans on the receiving end of a bite can expect anything from 'intense pain' to a feeling 'no worse than a wasp sting' (which is still pretty f*cking bad).

Such a choice! Just remember, these guys have got legs, and they know how to use them.

No one likes being nipped on the ass by an ant, but in Australia you're not so much nipped as viciously serrated by the hyper-aggressive bull or bulldog ant, which has a well-earned reputation as the world's most dangerous. Didn't you just know it would live here?

Australia is home to 90 species of the bastards, with the smaller varieties known as Jack Jumpers because they jump (yes, jump!) towards intruders, grab them with their jaws and then sting with their tail. Basically, stay indoors.

(Relatively) tiny but definitely deadly, *Myrmecia pyriformis* poses a serious, occasionally fatal threat to humans, causing anaphylactic shock and death. According to South Australia's Department of Respiratory Medicine, these ants probably kill far more people than we know, because many apparent heart-attack victims may in fact have being stung by a bull ant.

There are lots of dangerous creatures in this book, but you're looking at some of the meanest: these guys can kill. No bull.

#42 And *killer* ants!

#43

Our ticks can go from this... to THIS!

We're a nation of pet-lovers but in this land of myriad terrors, owning a dog or cat is never anything less than a horrifying experience. Snakes, spiders and cane toads all pose awful, everyday dangers to our little companions, but the most feared of all these monsters is so much smaller: a humble tick.

This being Australia, as well as harbouring 70 or so species of ticks doing what ticks normally do, we are also unlucky enough to have *Ixodes holocyclus*, better known as the paralysis tick. This repulsive creature pierces your pet's skin, feasts on its blood – usually around the head – and swells rapidly over four days. As it engorges, it injects a highly toxic saliva that can have fast and frightening results.

In animals, paralysis can set in fairly quickly and become so severe that your pet is unable to stand or move its head. Unless antiserum is given early, before signs are too advanced, coma and death usually follow. The best solution is daily checks, although of course these guys are easier to spot after the damage is done, once they're puffed up with blood.

And humans aren't free from their clutches. Those afflicted can experience rashes, headache, fever, weak limbs, partial facial paralysis and even anaphylactic shock. Yep, these tiny pests really suck. You'd be better off never leaving your living room, right?

THE O

Girt by sea. That's us. After all, our national anthem says so.

And we like to live close to it – almost 85 per cent of Australians reside less than 50 kilometres from the ocean, mostly somewhere between Cairns and Adelaide.

It's funny that all Aussies have a subconscious, not entirely rational fear of being munched by a shark – or a crocodile in the tropics – every time we go to the beach, yet almost zero awareness of the far bigger danger, rips.

Writing in *The Australian* in December 2015, Trent Dalton described a rip as 'a strong, narrow, seaward-bound liquid leviathan channelling water brought onshore by breaking waves back offshore at a speed of up to two metres per second, the pace of an Olympic swimmer'. Evocative stuff. These deadly, unpredictable killer water flows take on average 21 lives each year – more than from floods, bushfires, cyclones and shark attacks combined.

Okay, so if the sharks and crocs don't get you, the water itself will. But apart from that, it's all good, right? Ah, nope.

CEAN

Get a look at this poor chap checking out the (not in any way comprehensive) array of life-threatening options that await him if he foolishly decides to venture into the water.

Yes, the sun is shining, the sea looks a mesmerising shade of blue, but the list of Hazardous Marine Creatures that await should make any sensible person head straight for the safety of the nearest indoor public swimming pool.

There are literally dozens of dangerous (by which we mean deadly) options lurking beneath that apparently benign surface. Enter at your peril …

We have the BIGG deadly jellyfish

During marine stinger season, which runs from October to April, beaches across the top of Australia are closed, displaying scary, very visible warning signs for good reasons. This is one of them.

Australia's box jellyfish, or *Chironex fleckeri*, is considered the world's most venomous marine animal. Researchers from Hawaii's Department of Tropical Medicine have found that venom from the box jellyfish can lead to death within two to five minutes. The initial pain is so f*cking excruciatingly agonising that you will probably go into shock and drown BEFORE the full effect of the venom kicks in. If that's any consolation.

The size of a basketball, the box jelly has 40 or more 2-metre-long tentacles covered in stinging cells called nematocysts, which store and inject millions of little doses of venom upon contact with human skin. Box jellyfish have caused at least 79 deaths in Australia since 1883. Your best way of staying safe? Press 'play' on the oldest record in Oz: Stay Out Of The Water!

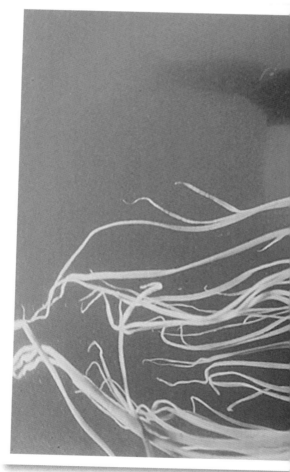

EST
on Earth

#44

OZ FACT

Queenslander Rachael Shardlow is lucky to be alive. In 2010, the 10-year-old was swimming in the Calliope River, several kilometres from the ocean, when she was stung by a box jellyfish. By the time her brother pulled her out she couldn't see or breathe; seconds later she lost consciousness. Incredibly, Rachael woke from her coma in the first 30 minutes and, after six weeks of treatment to the severe, burn-like lashes on her legs, she was allowed home. 'I don't know of anybody ... who has had such an extensive sting and has survived,' zoologist Jamie Seymour told UK paper *The Telegraph*.

#45
We have the *smallest* deadly jellyfish on Earth.

As if one basketball-sized lethal jellyfish wasn't enough, Australia's tropical waters are also home to a tiny potential killer with a punch 100 times more potent than a cobra.

Irukandjis, named after the Indigenous Yirrganydji people who live near Palm Cove in Far North Queensland, exploded into the public consciousness in 2002, when two tourists – a British man swimming off Hamilton Island and an American man snorkelling off Port Douglas – died after succumbing to the reactions of Irukandji stings. The twin tragedies are featured in Wendy Lewis's book *See Australia and Die*, almost certainly Tourism Australia's least favourite publication (well, until this one).

Irukandji syndrome is barely noticeable at first – some have described the sting as like a mozzie bite. Approximately 30 minutes later, however, the shit MASSIVELY hits the fan and 'a dreadful suite of symptoms kick in'. Imagine an electric drill powering its way into your lower back. Now add never-ending vomiting and nausea. Sounds like fun, right? How about waves of full-body cramps and temperatures so high that every millimetre of fluid is pouring out of your

body, soaking your bed sheets every 15 minutes? You cannot breathe, btw. You're also hyperventilating. And, through all this agony, all you can think is 'DOOM, DOOM'.

One victim described the feeling as 'on a pain scale of one to 10, it rated between 15 and 20'. Did we mention that most locals in the tropics never go in the water?

OZ FACT
Among the array of horrifying symptoms, most striking to observers is a 'feeling of impending doom'. According to jellyfish taxonomist Lisa-Anne Gershwin, 'Patients believe they're going to die and they're so certain of it that they'll actually beg their doctors to kill them just to get it over with.'

#46

We have snakes in the *sea*. Yep. Sea snakes.

You probably thought that Australia has enough venomous snakes on land to cut the ocean a bit of slack right? Well, sorry, Australia's 30-odd species of killer sea snake had other ideas.

The most common of these, the yellow-bellied sea snake, is highly venomous. While its fangs are very short (only 1.5 millimetres) and so only capable of injecting a small dose of venom, that venom is highly f*cking toxic. Symptoms of a bite include muscle pain and stiffness, drooping eyelids, drowsiness and vomiting, total paralysis and death.

OZ FACT
Most sea snake bites occur on fishing trawlers in the Tropics, when the snakes are accidentally hauled in with the catch. No deaths have been recorded in Australian waters. But maybe that's because dead people don't talk.

To its achievements of being damn attractive and bloody deadly, the yellow-bellied sea snake also adds the distinction of being the world's most widely ranging snake. It spends its life in the pelagic region of the ocean (neither sea floor nor surface) and never has to slither onto land. So to encounter one of these beauties you would have to be seriously unlucky, having one swept against you in the surf or picking up one that had been washed ashore.

Sea snakes are mostly found in tropical seas but are often pushed further south by tropical storms – and, like any Aussie, they're particularly worth avoiding when they're tired, far from home and grumpy. According to zoologist Jamie Seymour, associate professor at James Cook University, 'the majority of sea snakes are very placid'. Aw, they're chilled killers.

We have the only species that's *fatal*

Apparently docile and timid, this teeny-weeny octopus, just a few centimetres long, is an inoffensive dark-brown sort of colour until you piss him off. Then the vivid blue rings that suddenly come into focus give you a very clear warning: Back. The. F*ck. Off.

If you choose to ignore this clear signal, or if you've just unwittingly tramped over his home in your bare feet, your new mate will make his presence very clearly felt, injecting a venom that quickly goes to work on your respiratory system.

As Andrew Burnell, marine parks officer with the NSW Department of Environment and Heritage, puts it: 'You can be wide awake and looking around and completely conscious, but it paralyses your breathing muscles.' Welcome to blue-ringed octopus hell, where no one can hear you scream.

What happens next? Well, there is no antivenom, which means you have to get yourself to hospital, sit on a ventilator and deal with it. For 15 agonising hours.

While the blue-ringed octopus has long had a fearsome reputation for its ability to kill humans in minutes (although there are just two recorded fatalities), it was only in 2009 that a study showed that all octopuses and cuttlefish are venomous – it's just that the big ones aren't so mean.

If you're planning on going fishing, follow the excellent advice of Perth recreational fisho Steve Hart, who posted on Facebook: 'Unless you want to give your smelly mate mouth-to-mouth until he gets emergency assistance, you might want to start wearing gloves and footwear on the boat.'

# of octopus to humans.

#48 Just because it's pretty doesn't mean it won't *kill* you.

By now you have probably drawn the entirely correct conclusion that the words 'venomous' and 'Australia' are almost always found in the same sentence.

Lists of deadly animals are usually ranked by their danger and proximity to humans. But how about if Australia's most deadly were ranked by their venom alone?

As you'd expect, our old mate the inland taipan snake is at #1, with a bite that packs enough venom to kill more than 100 people. But you probably won't guess the creature occupying #2 on *Australian Geographic*'s Most Venomous list. And nope, it's not the eastern brown snake or box jellyfish. Because Australia's second most venomous creature is the ickle cone shell (*Conus geographus*), which has the ability to kill 15 people with one sting from its harpoon-like tooth.

Packing neurotoxins that affect vision and speech, the cone shell or cone snail has only been responsible for one recorded death, way back in 1935, but that doesn't mean he couldn't cause f*cking carnage if he wanted. So before you say, 'Oh, pretty shell', and reach for this patterned poisoner, THINK! Because this guy's venom can cause paralysis, respiratory failure and, you guessed it, death.

The pretty designs of cone shells often attract the attention of unsuspecting beachcombers, especially kids. But a cone shell on the beach will likely still have a living animal inside; one in the water almost certainly will. So remember: if it's a cone, LEAVE IT ALONE!

So snails, jellyfish and cuttlefish make Australia's oceans a pretty scary place, right? Still, at least there isn't a f*cking dangerous fish too. Oh wait, of course there is. And not just a little bit dangerous either.

Our reef stonefish is the most poisonous fish on the planet, and a perfectly camouflaged killing machine. Okay, he's not specifically out to kill YOU, but because he looks exactly like a rock or piece of coral, he's a pretty easy thing to step on and, if you do, those 13 sharp, venomous dorsal spines along his back can induce excruciating pain and severe nausea. You know the drill – get to a doctor fast.

Just to make things worse, stonefish are not only impossibly ugly but they can also survive out of the water for up to 24 hours. So if for some reason you're planning on wandering around on exposed reef flats or wading around in shallow water, wear some VERY thick-soled shoes.

Funnily enough, for such a big (up to 35 centimetres), unpleasant-looking dude, the stonefish is remarkably fast when it comes to grabbing a snack. He waits for his prey to swim past, then strikes with lightning speed that requires high-speed camera equipment to capture the process.

Even the *ugly* ones want you dead.

#49

#50 Do we *need* to say more than 'croc'?

In Queensland and the Northern Territory, where stingers are a major hindrance to our ocean frolics, authorities provide stinger nets, allowing people to swim somewhere jellyfish-free. Unfortunately, they don't keep everything *out*.

Exhibit A: Children swimming at Etty Bay in Far North Queensland were told in no uncertain terms to 'get out of the f*cking water!' when a crocodile was spotted lounging on the float that marks the edge of the stinger enclosure. Judging by the expression on his face, he no doubt found this great sport.

Despite the efforts of Queensland Parks and Wildlife Service rangers, the larrikin crocodile was never caught. Surf lifesavers reopened the beach the next day as the croc was nowhere to be seen – we can only hope he headed back over the float and is today telling his family about the 'ones that got away'.

Exhibit B: A 4-metre crocodile closed Broome's Cable Beach for a day and spent the arvo catching the waves (Aussies do love a surf). Sharon Scoble, who took this amazing pic from the shore, said, 'He was a big boy – his head was huge. It was absolutely awesome.' She did admit, however, that 'it wouldn't have been so awesome if I was swimming and noticed it'.

OZ FACT Open beaches are not a favoured habitat of salties, and it is very rare to see one at the beach, where the clear water and sandy bottom make it difficult for the croc to hide. These guys much prefer murky river mouths and mangrove swamps.

You've probably noticed that just like everything else in Australia, the nation's politics are pretty barmy too. Five prime ministers in five years? Check. A prime minister booted out of his own seat at the end of 11 glorious years? Check. An elected prime minister booted out by an unelected governor-general acting in the name of a monarch 17,000 kilometres away in London? Check.

But of all #AusPol's crazy tales, none is curiouser or more fabulously, tragically Australian than the bizarre loss of our 18th PM Harold Holt, who disappeared while swimming in 'high and fierce surf' near Portsea, Victoria, on 17 December 1967.

Despite a massive search operation – the biggest in the nation's history – involving police, navy divers and air force helicopters, his body was never found. Yep, Australia actually lost a prime minister.

Holt was a strong, experienced swimmer taking a dip at one of his favourite beaches, and according to his biographer, Tom Frame, he had 'incredible powers of endurance underwater'. But, suffering from a shoulder injury, he'd ignored his doctor's advice not to swim.

Holt is famously remembered by the Harold Holt Memorial Swimming Centre in Glen Iris, Melbourne – an irony not lost on author Bill Bryson, who recalled seeing it and thinking 'what a wonderful country'. After all, we coined the rhyming slang 'to do a Harold Holt', which means 'to do a bolt' or make a quick exit.

Our ocean is so *mysterious*, it's even claimed a prime minister. #51

Fewer than 400,000 people live in Outback Australia, with only 180,000 in the arid zone, less than 0.1 person per sq km.

Of the more than 200 countries the World Bank ranks by population density, only Mongolia has fewer people per square kilometre. That's a helluva lot of empty space. Devoid of rain, Australia's interior comprises about 45 per cent of hot desert or treeless grasslands, neither environment at all conducive to supporting even very small human populations.

Antarctica apart, Australia is the driest continent, and the nation's remote areas and deserts are among the most unforgiving on Earth. Temperatures can soar close to 50°C in the summer and drop below freezing to minus 10°C during winter nights.

The struggle to survive in the desert lands has long been central to Australia's identity, the harsh interior seen from the beginning as the embryonic nation's Wild West, the conquest of the empty 'dead heart' a defining goal for the earliest European settlers.

But of course the outback was never empty: Indigenous people have been living in the desert for tens of thousands of years, passing down land-management techniques and water knowledge through the generations. Today, government researchers are desperately trying to capture priceless Aboriginal land-management knowledge before it is lost forever.

So what is out there? Well, lots of mines – the outback is extremely rich in reserves of iron, aluminium and uranium ores. And gold, if only you could find it. There are also plenty of kangaroos, camels, dingoes, birds and, natch, the occasional snake. Plus 28 million cattle.

At 6 million acres (24,000 square kilometres), Anna Creek in South Australia is the world's biggest cattle station. How big? Bigger than Belgium or Israel! Yep, we've got farms bigger than entire countries! Just hope the owners don't need to borrow a cup of sugar from the neighbours.

#52

Space is *closer* than the nearest town.

How big is the outback? Massive. How empty? Desolate. For instance, there's a remote spot at the western edge of WA's Gunbarrel Highway where a road sign reveals that the nearest town, Warburton, is 493 kilometres away.

Nothing extraordinary about that, right? Wrong. Turns out the Kármán line, which commonly represents the boundary between Earth's atmosphere and outer space, is a mere 100 kilometres above sea level. That's FIVE TIMES closer than Warburton.

This sign is on the outskirts of Carnegie Station, Western Australia, a very, very long way from anywhere – the nearest city is Perth, 1320 kilometres away. It's the last fuel stop for 500 k's too, so you'd better make sure you have adequate supplies. Check your tyres, check your oil and water, and maybe don't watch *Wolf Creek* before you set off – or if you do, follow the advice of the movie's tagline, which sensibly asks: 'How can you be found when no-one knows you're missing?'

Beyond the very obvious – don't set off into the world's biggest wilderness with a couple of bottles of water and no satellite phone – here's the golden rule of survival out here: Let. Somebody. Know. When you're going, where you're going, when you expect to be back.

THINK! Stay alive!

#53 Outback *survival* stories are few and far between.

We mentioned *Wolf Creek*, which is loosely based on the real-life murders of tourists by two of Australia's most notorious killers, Ivan Milat and Bradley Murdoch. Sadly, Australia is known for its psychos just as much as its deadly animals.

But the Outback itself features almost as much in travellers' tales, claiming around 40 lives a year.

Wilderness expert Bob Cooper, author of *Outback Survival*, has been training people how to stay alive in the Outback for decades. 'The decisions you make in the first few hours are critical to life and death,' he says. 'Survival is a mind game first of all. If you don't die, it's because you think you're going to survive.'

Alaskan Robert Bogucki survived 43 days in WA's Great Sandy Desert by eating plants and flowers after his food ran out. Police called off the search after 12 days, but Bogucki's parents called in specialist US trackers, who eventually found him, dazed, in a creek.

Wearing only a T-shirt, shorts, cap and thongs, 62-year-old hunter Reg Foggerdy disappeared while pursuing a feral camel. Without any water, he survived for six days lying in the shade beneath a tree and eating black ants, until searchers found him.

British backpacker Sam Woodhead got lost for three days after going for a run near the remote Queensland cattle station he was working on during his gap year. After drinking his litre of water in the first hour, he survived by drinking the saline solution from his contact lenses.

Diabetic, insulin-dependent German Daniel Dudzisz went missing near Longreach in remote Queensland where, stranded by floods, he survived for two weeks by eating flies. He joked to his rescuers he'd have never gone hungry due to the sheer number of flies available.

Flies *outnumber* people by about a gazillion to one. #54

Okay, so the desolation and ferocious heat are most likely to kill you, but there's a very good chance that the f*cking flies will drive you batshit insane first.

Drawn to sweat, saliva, blood and your eyes, Australia's bush fly (*Musca vetustissima*) is found in its billions in the Outback. A dung fly, it's attracted to large mammals (yep, that's us) for nourishment, and lays its eggs in cow shit – or human shit if it can find it (camping – think about it). Which is why it's a very good idea to keep flies' crap-covered feet away from your face.

Bush flies breed in massive numbers when there's a drought, which is another of Australia's common crazy-ass afflictions.

Unfortunately, drought affects the dung beetles that were introduced to kill bush flies, making them inactive and therefore bad at their job of crap dispersion (the best fly deterrent). Slack dung beetles means more flies which, in turn, means more pissed-off people.

The ridiculous corked hat is a stereotypical Aussie souvenir that's long been associated with keeping away flies, although there's little evidence that cork hats have ever been widely used, let alone useful. Visit Uluru between October and March and you'll see tourists sporting the modern equivalent: the equally silly-looking, but at least rather effective, mesh veil.

Anyone not protecting themselves will be busy employing the 'Australian salute', a uniquely local way of waving your hand to stop flies landing on your face or entering your nose or mouth.

#55

And then there are the ones the signs don't warn you about. When you're not avoiding millions of suicidal kangaroos and kamikaze members of the world's largest wild camel herd, take care to watch for dangerous rogue creatures like this feral pig, who went on a booze-fuelled rampage in a campsite in WA's Pilbara region in 2013.

According to staff from Main Roads WA, the pig, nicknamed Swino (because Australia, because nicknames), drank up to 18 tinnies at the DeGrey River rest area, then started ripping apart the bins.

'It was in the middle of the night,' reported a camper. 'These people camping opposite us heard this crunching of the can … and there he was scrunching away. Some other people saw him running around their vehicle being chased by a cow.' Just another wild night in the Australian Outback.

Sadly, Swino met his end in a car accident a month later. But to avoid your own curly camping tale, make sure your food and booze are safely stashed when you're camping in remote areas, because a) there are an estimated 23 million feral pigs and b) they're actually not the most dangerous creature that could be messing with your rubbish. (Snakes. Remember snakes?!)

Beer-loving beasts can wreak *havoc* on your campsite.

OZ FACT

Australia has huge populations of feral invaders, including camels, cane toads, cats and water buffalo. Despite the WA government's 1700-kilometre rabbit-proof fence, built between 1901 and 1907, feral rabbits successfully colonised habitats right across Australia. By the 1920s the bunny population – first introduced with a dozen rabbits in Geelong – had swollen to ten billion! After the introduction of the myxomatosis virus in the 1950s it was reduced to an estimated 200 million.

The road's dead straight. There are no trees for as far as the eye can see. For the next 96 kilometres – and probably the 960 kilometres beyond that too – you're going to need to keep your eyes peeled for stray camels, wombats and kangaroos. Possibly all at once.

Good luck making it to the other side. An accurate estimate of Australia's kangaroo population is hard to find – approximately 25 million at last count, though the government stopped listing them online in 2011 – but they grow steadily in normal years and crash rapidly in droughts.

Then you've got about half a million camels and who knows how many wombats ...

If you're driving by day you're sure to see shedloads of kangaroos and wombats, but sadly they'll be lying dead and bloated beside the road, often with wedge-tailed eagles, Australia's largest bird of prey, enjoying the feast.

Drive at night and you'll understand why there's so much roadkill. Of course, driving at a sensible speed will help you avoid encounters with wildlife. But if an animal does appear on the road in front of you,

brake firmly, not suddenly, and hit it if necessary (easier said than done).

Don't try to swerve as you're likely to run onto the gravel verge, lose control and roll your vehicle. If you do hit something, clean it up if you can so scavengers aren't put in danger as well. Better still – don't drive at night.

#56

Native wildlife exist solely to ruin your *road trip.*

OZ FACT Australia being Australia, there's always a lighter side (or darker, depending on how you look at it) to every situation. 'You Kill It, We Grill It': that's the promise at Darwin's Roadkill Café, which offers kangaroo and wallaby satay, buffalo or camel sausages and a possum or mutton bird special among its treats.

NULLARBOR PLAIN
EASTERN END OF TREELESS PLAIN

OZ FACT

Running perpendicular to the Eyre Highway is a single sealed road spanning the interior between Australia's north and south coasts. Known as the Stuart Highway (after explorer John McDouall Stuart) or The Track, it stretches 2834 kilometres from Darwin in the Northern Territory to Port Augusta in South Australia.

Roads are mind-numbingly *dull*.

Stretching 14,500 kilometres right around Australia, Highway One is one of the world's great drives. But in what other nation would the main highway proudly boast a section still unsealed in 2016?!

The Australian landscape has rainforest, rugged ranges and surprisingly alpine areas, yet the vast majority of the country's interior is relentlessly flat and featureless. Which makes for some challenging driving. In the Outback, one of the biggest killers is fatigue: huge distances with unvarying, unchanging landscapes have a habit of zzzzzzzz. Yep, you get it. Drivers have been known to become so mesmerised by the straights that they forget to slow down when a corner eventually comes, and they drive into the ditch.

The big message is, take a break if you have sore or heavy eyes, fuzzy vision, hallucinations or start wandering across the road. Drivers are advised not to travel more than 10 hours a day, which sounds insane but is the bare minimum necessary to circumnavigate the nation in less than 30 days. Yep, Australia is f*cking massive, mate.

Stretching over vast, treeless wastes, the Eyre Highway across the Nullarbor Plain is Australia's craziest road. Named after the first European explorer to cross the plain, this 1675-kilometre highway opened in 1942 and was finally sealed in 1976. It includes the longest section of straight road in Australia, a totally ridiculous 145.6 k's with absolutely no turns, known as the '90 Mile Straight'.

You probably fell asleep just reading that sentence. Imagine trying to drive it. Order a very large, very strong coffee. And pump up the tunes.

Think of the poor guys who have to negotiate those endless roads for a living. The trucks that carry iron ore from our mines to the coast are so f*cking massive they're known as road trains. These beasts are truly gigantic, the largest and heaviest in the world.

At a bare minimum, road trains are at least 36.5 metres in length, including two or three trailers. With the right permit, drivers can pull four trailers, making a total length of 53.5 metres. On private mining company roads, the trucks get even longer.

You know that heart-in-mouth feeling when you're overtaking a big truck on a single-lane highway? Are you going to make it? Now magnify that by four: 53.5 metres is a lot of road to cover. And 86 wheels, supporting 200 tonnes, take a lot of braking, which means these truckies ain't stopping for anyone!

So if you're on an unsealed road and see a road train coming, GET OFF THE ROAD – they kick up a shitload of rocks and generate their own dust storms.

Dramatics aside, anyone who's driven in the Outback knows that truckies are hugely considerate, safe drivers. But we can't help wondering if somewhere out there Australia is cultivating its own version of Steven Spielberg's 1971 cult-classic *Duel*, in which a monster road train tried to kill the movie's protagonist. Food for thought.

If you don't fall asleep or get lost, it's likely a road train will *kill* you.

#58

OZ FACT
The world record for hauling the longest road train was set at Clifton, Queensland, in 2006 by a single prime mover pulling 112 trailers that stretched 1474m. Try passing that!

Australia's mining industry has made the Outback a *death trap*. #59

We know the road trains transporting the finds from Australia's mines are dangerous, but what about the mines themselves? As this sign suggests, when it comes to mine shafts, Australia is one big booby trap.

Home to some of the world's richest minerals and precious metals, Australia boasts some pretty impressive mines, such as our largest open-cut gold mine, the Super Pit at Kalgoorlie in WA, which is 3.5 kilometres long, 1.5 kilometres wide and 570 metres deep, and can be seen from space. But most Australian mines are significantly smaller, and more dangerous.

Coober Pedy in remote South Australia is described as the 'opal capital of the world'. It's also surrounded by more than 250,000 abandoned mine shafts. These 'evils of the Outback' are supposed to be filled in or covered with a metal sheet after mining operations cease, but in practice many remain open, just waiting to snare unsuspecting victims. Sadly, there are plenty.

Like everywhere else in Australia, read the signs. They say DANGER for a reason. Don't think you can go off-piste without something very bad happening. This is Straya and, if it can, the worst-case scenario will almost certainly eventuate.

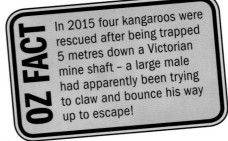

OZ FACT In 2015 four kangaroos were rescued after being trapped 5 metres down a Victorian mine shaft – a large male had apparently been trying to claw and bounce his way up to escape!

Here's an Aussie bloke doing what Aussie blokes do best: building dreams where all the signs say dreams shouldn't be built. For 60,000 years or so, homo sapiens have been building a society on a continent engineered to make survival impossible.

Australia is home to the world's oldest living culture, with storylines mapped out tens of thousands of years ago criss-crossing the land. Since 1788, a bewildering variety of humans from all corners of the planet have built a modern Australia from the dust up.

Less than 1 per cent of Australia's population lives in the arid zone that covers more than 81 per cent of the continent. And no wonder – this is one of the driest places on Earth, a vast land that, effectively, is permanently in drought.

But the Australian spirit demands that Australians defy reality. Which is why there's a golf course in Coober Pedy – a town that only gets 155 millimetres of rain a year, over just 19 days. An 18-hole golf course in a town with no water. A golf course with no bloody grass! Go home, Australia, you're drunk.

OZ FACT

As if a golf course in the desert wasn't crazy enough, the Eyre Highway Operators Association went one step further in 2006, opening a 1365-kilometre long, 18-hole golf course straddling two states. You tee off in Kalgoorlie, Western Australia, play a couple of holes, drive 100 kilometres or so to the next roadhouse, play another hole, and keep going all the way to Ceduna in South Australia. Make sure you have lots of balls, because out of bounds stretches forever.

There's a *grassless* bloody golf course!

#60

FIRES

Let's get serious. There's nothing funny about fires. And Australia is a land truly shaped by fire.

One of the remarkable things about the array of WTF creatures that call the Land Down Under home is that they evolved over millions of years on a continent that goes out of its way to kill every living thing on a regular basis. Australia's fires, floods and storms are nothing to laugh about – as this chapters show, they've caused unimaginable catastrophe and tragedy.

In October 2013, ferocious fires threatened Sydney and caused chaos in surrounding areas. Warm, windy weather fuelled fierce conflagrations and, at their peak, more than 100 blazes were burning across New South Wales, the worst fires to hit the state since the 1960s.

Late one evening, Channel 7 television cameraman Paul Walker captured a bunch of volunteer firies taking a break after a day of fighting life-threatening blazes near Redhead Beach, south of Newcastle, their chilled demeanour epitomising the Australian spirit in the face of adversity.

Australians collectively exhibit a wonderful defiance in the face of the worst Mother Nature can throw at us. It's as if, as a nation, we acknowledge that the beauty of our environment is inexorably linked to its rare power, and if that power sometimes strikes out and hurts us, that's the price we pay for living in paradise. It's something that's hard-baked into the Australian national character. Which is just as well ...

#61 Our most famous tree is also our most *flammable*.

'Bushfires are part of the Australian landscape,' reports *Australian Geographic* magazine. 'They have been around for an estimated 60 million years and they are a regular cycle in our climate.'

Fire has forged Australia's national character – our worst nightmares feature fire fronts marching up ridges towards us, or racing dangerously across paddocks, high as three-storey buildings. But it does seem just a little unfair/typical that our very landscape has evolved to feed the beast.

The eucalypt, our most successful tree, is perfectly designed to power bushfires. Its fallen leaves create thick, combustible carpets, its bark peels off in streamers that bring the fire back up into the foliage, and the fragrant oil for which it is known is incredibly flammable. In fact, eucalypts have been described as 'gasoline trees', but their contrary charms don't end there. Ironically, the very trees that can cause all this mayhem have adapted to survive, and even thrive, in wildfire conditions. Their seed capsules open when burned and release seedlings that just love a dip in ash-heavy soil.

Evolution, eh? Makes you think.

OZ FACT While occasional bushfires in populous south-eastern Australia receive extensive media coverage, much bigger fires in the desert or savannah country are annual events. One NT fire burning in late 2007 covered 60,000 square kilometres, an area two-thirds the size of Tasmania, yet wasn't even reported by local media, let alone nationally. Out of sight, out of mind?

#62

Indigenous people coped with bushfires for 50,000 years – what's the *problem* now?

For tens of thousands of years, right across the continent, Indigenous people employed fire to manage the land and unlock its value.

Plants and bush foods grew immediately after fire, camping spots were cleared of snakes, goannas were smoked out of holes. Indigenous people set fire fronts a kilometre wide to flush out kangaroos, and much bigger fires to clean up country. Fire sparked smoking ceremonies; burning native plants warded off bad spirits. In fact, some Indigenous languages have more than 100 different words for fire.

Unfortunately, a lot of Indigenous knowledge of handling fire on the most combustible continent on Earth has almost entirely been lost. At the same time, fires are getting worse. As CSIRO's Dr Garry Cook puts it, 'Since European settlement, fires in the north have increased in size and severity. This has threatened biodiversity as well as increased greenhouse gas emissions.'

So as fires have intensified, there's been renewed recognition that Australia's fire managers need to go back to basics and learn from Indigenous people.

According to the University of Tasmania's Professor David Bowman, the sustainable way Indigenous people managed fire for tens of thousands of years 'shows that human beings can co-exist with a highly flammable environment'. Our challenge, he says, is to devise new ways inspired by the principle 'that human beings and flammable landscapes can exist harmoniously'.

#63 People try to *fight*, not flee, dangerous fires.

Black Friday, 13 January 1939: Australia's third worst bushfires in history. Victoria was in the grip of a record heatwave following drought conditions and water shortages. Hundreds of fires raged out of control, triggered by the high temperatures and strong winds.

'About midday the smoke started to appear,' recalled survivor Brian Lloyd. 'Next thing, across the river from our place, we saw a fire come up from the north heading south like giant red kangaroos leaping through the tops of the trees, a terrible sight, a frightening sight. There were tins of kerosene and ancient ammunition going off, like geysers. The place was our life and it all went up in flames.'

Basil Barnard, 22 at the time, was working at the local mill, determined to keep business going. 'We must have been mad,' he recalled, talking to the ABC's *7:30 Report* 64 years later. 'We were being showered with burning leaves, burnt leaves and twigs. But, you know, your job was there and you had to do it.'

Barnard was one of the lucky ones and escaped in the last car out. Meanwhile, residents fought to defend their homes. Some volunteers had already been fighting fires for days, using nothing more than beaters and branches.

Ahead of the fire, birds dropped dead on the road, 15 centimetres deep in places. The firestorm came through like a hurricane, ripping sheets of corrugated iron from houses and sending them flying through the air.

In one town, just 14 of 143 houses remained. More than 1000 homes were destroyed and 69 sawmills burned. The fires claimed 71 lives in total.

OZ FACT People were found to have deliberately or carelessly contributed to the Black Friday fires by burning off for land clearing, lighting campfires, conducting inappropriate sawmill operations and causing domestic fires. In the subsequent Royal Commission, Judge Stretton described the fires as 'the most disastrous forest calamity the State of Victoria has ever known'.

Destructive, *deadly* fires can rage hundreds of kilometres apart.

#64

Ash Wednesday, 16 February 1983: Australia's second worst bushfires. After a prolonged drought on the back of a strong El Niño climate system, with rainfall levels as little as half the previous record lows, southern Australia was bone-dry, a tinderbox of dangerous fuel waiting to spark. Then climate and weather combined to smash Victoria and SA at the same time.

By midday on Ash Wednesday, in 43°C temperatures with winds gusting to 100 kilometres per hour, multiple fires broke out, many caused by sparks from short-circuiting power lines and some, sadly, deliberately lit by people. A disastrous dry wind change just before nightfall altered the direction, speed and intensity of the fires, breaking containment lines and cutting off escape routes.

'It was like a hailstorm, but it wasn't hail,' recalled Eric Bumpstead, then captain of the Upper Beaconsfield fire brigade. 'It was red-hot coals and twigs and all [of that] was burning you.'

In the midst of this devastating maelstrom, road surfaces bubbled and sand liquefied to glass as towns were obliterated in minutes. 'Just this bloody great force. It wasn't fire by itself. It wasn't just the wind. It was something different to that … a monster.'

By the time the fire was brought under control, 47 people were dead in Victoria and 28 in SA. More than 3700 buildings were destroyed or damaged and 2545 people lost their homes. Approximately 340,000 sheep and 18,000 cattle were dead or later destroyed.

Aussies fight to *save*

#65
their animals.

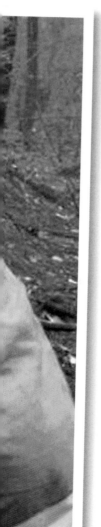

It was an image that captivated the nation and although it occurred a week before the Black Saturday fires of 7 February 2009, it became forever associated with them, a symbol of hope to be taken from Australia's darkest hours.

Fire fighter David Tree and his crew found Sam the koala during backburning operations when they were 'blacking out' (making sure a contained or checked fire doesn't restart). Tree saw the bewildered animal, called for some water and offered her his bottle to drink from. The heartwarming film even shows Sam letting him pat her and hold her paw.

Sam was later taken to the Southern Ash Wildlife Centre in Rawson, where she was treated for second-degree burns and rehabilitated. Her story fascinated international media, including CNN and The New York Times, and the video of David Tree helping her was viewed more than 1.4 million times on YouTube.

Slow-moving, tree-dwelling koalas are some of the worst bushfire casualties, and the internet has its fair share of koala-saving stories. In 2015, the International Fund for Animal Welfare called for people to make 'koala mittens' (it even provided a pattern), to place on the burnt paws of animals who'd been harmed in bushfires. The charity was inundated with mittens and has now asked animal-loving sewers to try their hands at pouches for orphaned joeys.

As for the ongoing problem of bushfires in Australia, we'll leave you with David Tree's words upon first seeing Sam: 'How much can a koala bear?'

#66 On Australia's *darkest* day, 'stay or go' was a death sentence.

Black Saturday, 7 February 2009: Australia's all-time worst bushfires. The day everything that could go wrong did. The day record high temperatures of 46.4°C on the back of a prolonged heatwave and drought combined with high winds of up to 100 kilometres per hour to create a conflagration of 400 fires across Victoria that killed 173 people, with two-thirds trapped in their own homes.

Analysis of 1983's Ash Wednesday, where many who defended their homes survived while 17 highly trained firefighters perished fighting the blazes, contributed to the belief that it was safer for residents to be in their homes than out on the roads. The 'Stay or Go' policy (sometimes described as 'Fight or Flee') that resulted was also based on research into 'civilian' bushfire fatalities since 1900. That research concluded that 'late evacuation is the most common activity at the time of death'.

But in the face of this overwhelming disaster, the official policy – 'Prepare, Stay and Defend or Leave Early' – proved dire, with warnings and evacuation procedures terribly inadequate. The average speed of the fires was 12 kilometres per hour, but in some cases fires travelled up to six times that speed, or 1.2 kilometres a minute. The energy released from the fires is said to have been the equivalent of 1500 Hiroshima atomic bombs, with the radiant heat enough to kill people 400 metres away.

In the aftermath of this, Australia's most terrible day, which destroyed 2100 homes and displaced 7562 people, the nation's entire approach to fighting fire was challenged.

After 155 day of hearings, the Royal Commission recommended sweeping changes, including a 'comprehensive approach to evacuation' with 'emergency evacuations' when doing so would provide a greater level of protection.

It gets so f*cking hot that *tornadoes* are actually fire tornadoes.

#67

Summer temperatures in Australia's centre can soar close to 50°C. Combined with strong winds and fire, this can create a uniquely scary proposition: a tornado of whirling fire.

In 2012 film-maker Chris Tangey captured truly incredible footage of a rare firenado near Curtin Springs cattle station in the Northern Territory, which sent weather experts into a spin. 'It sounded like a jet fighter,' Tangey told the *NT News*, 'yet there wasn't a breath of wind where we were. It was like a stage show. You would have paid $1000 a head if you knew it was about to happen.'

Tangey simply couldn't believe what he was seeing, and nor could people around the world. Media outlets went into full OMG mode: 'A startling phenomenon … nabbed the world's attention … extraordinary … just look at this swirling column of fire … a rare natural spectacular.'

So, fire tornado?! How does that happen? According to CSIRO fire researcher Dr Andrew Sullivan, for such a vortex to form a 'shear' must be present, which involves one air flow (a prevailing fire or wind) coming perpendicular to another. 'If there is already a shear present, whirls will form regardless of the size of the fire. If there isn't a shear present, then larger fires will tend to induce them,' Sullivan told *Australian Geographic* magazine.

'Depending on the intensity of the fire, you can get updrafts. This forms a shear layer moving in two directions that induces a vortex.'

OZ FACT Fire tornadoes commonly arise during flash burns (a sudden, intense fire) and are very powerful. Dr Sullivan has seen logs thrown substantial distances. 'The key aim for flash-burn operators is to not allow enough heat to be generated for the fire whirls to form.' That's some KPI.

Nowhere in Australia is safe, even the capital.

#68

Before Tom Bates captured a fire tornado on video, the general consensus by scientists was that the phenomenon didn't exist. But on 18 January 2003, nature sent that theory up in smoke.

Ten days earlier, a huge lightning storm had sparked blazes in the ACT and large fires had been moving inexorably towards the outskirts of Canberra, 'the Bush Capital' surrounded by forested mountains. On the fateful day, the situation quickly turned catastrophic: by 9 am residents in the city's western suburbs were reporting burning embers; by 2.45 pm the ACT's chief minister had declared a state of emergency.

Less than an hour later, homes were being destroyed. 'The houses were alight, there were massive trees just torn out of the ground and dumped,' said Stephen Wilkes of the ACT Parks and Conservation Service. 'What kept coming to my mind was a tornado.' In the aftermath, the devastation baffled scientists: it was clear that the worst damage was due to something more savage than an ordinary fire. Houses suffered severe wind damage. The capital was ravaged, and four lives lost.

No such thing as a firenado? Unprecedented footage soon set the record straight: 'I've never in my life seen anything like it,' said Tom. 'It's got to be ripping poor bastards' houses up. Holy Jesus, this is bad news. It's like a tornado, like a big fireball tornado.'

As researchers pieced it together, no other explanation fitted: Canberra had been hit by a fire tornado. Beginning to the west of the city, a 25-kilometre path had cut a distinctive trail of destruction, centred on a vortex a kilometre wide that uprooted trees and burned through suburbs at extraordinary speeds of up to 250 kilometres per hour.

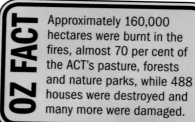

OZ FACT Approximately 160,000 hectares were burnt in the fires, almost 70 per cent of the ACT's pasture, forests and nature parks, while 488 houses were destroyed and many more were damaged.

In the face of *danger*, Aussies will always find the funny.

Nothing says 'Australia's weather is totally f*cked' like the fact that our fire danger system doesn't stop at 'extreme'. Seeing one of these warning signs for the first time, visitors are baffled: the danger rating jumps straight from a not-quite benign low-moderate to high, and then rapidly onwards to catastrophic.

While 89 per cent of Australians live in urban areas supposedly safe from fire, the destructive blazes that hit the nation's capital, Canberra, in 2003 were a stark warning that, really, everywhere is vulnerable.

Now prominent across Australia, the National Fire Danger Rating System was adopted after 2009's Black Saturday disaster. It's unambiguous: if you're in the path of a catastrophic fire, you're in the wrong place.

If this sign went any higher it would say APOCALYPTIC, but that would be superfluous, because the sign itself would be on fire.

Of course, being Australia, a picture like this draws its comforting share of take-the-piss comments. 'I feel sorry for the guy who has to drive out there and point the arrow towards Code Red,' says one.

Actually, the new boards are apparently electronic and controlled remotely – though the technology has been known to break down on hot days (!).

Other suggestions for the final warning include 'Why Are You Even Reading this Sign?' and the simple yet dignified 'You're F*cked'.

We quite like the true-blue, no bullsh*t rating system suggested by one punter:

She's Right.

Bit of a Worry.

Strewth, Doesn't Look Good.

Pretty Fuckin' High, Mate.

Yeah, Na, Ya F*cked.

F*ck this, I'm Off to the Pub.

FIRE DANGER RATING TODAY

HIGH • VERY HIGH • SEVERE • EXTREME

LOW-MODERATE • CATASTROPHIC

· PREPARE. ACT. SURVIVE. ·

FLOO

When it rains in Australia, it pours. Don't let any Pom try to tell you that the UK gets more rain.

Total bullshit: Sydney's annual rainfall (1337 millimetres) is double London's (594 millimetres). Yes, Australia is the driest continent and predominantly defined by fire and drought. But when the heavens open it's like a biblical flood.

In 2011, Queensland was blown away, literally, by one hell of a wet season. Boasting (if you can boast about these things) category 5 cyclones and unprecedented floods, 2011 ranked as Australia's wettest year since 1788, and most likely since at least 1488.

In January 2016, record rain was smashing NSW's Hunter region, with more than 1400 requests for help from flash flooding in one morning. But in an average year, everywhere east of the Great Dividing Range sees some pretty solid rain. In bust years, particularly those coinciding with the La Niña weather system and/or the end of long droughts, the deluge can cause massive destruction and affect the entire economy – 2011 saw banana prices spike to $20 per kilo nationwide, and a $1.8 billion flood levy was passed by the Federal Government to provide reconstruction funds for Queensland.

But then, as a bonus, Lake Eyre fills, the Murray flows and the reservoirs are finally full.

Between 1852 and 2011, at least 951 Australians were killed by floods, another 1326 were injured, and the cost of damage reached an estimated $4.76 billion.

Sitting on a flood plain in a subtropical climate, Brisbane is a) a beautifully situated city and b) a city situated in a bloody ridiculous place. If you were deliberately looking to build a major metropolis in a particularly precarious location, you really couldn't do much better than the banks of the Brisbane River.

You're at the mercy of unpredictable storms, located in a spot where water can't drain fast when volumes rise rapidly, and surrounded by flat suburbs beyond the river banks to increase the devastation. So hats off to Surveyor General John Oxley, who first charted the Brissie in 1824 and recommended it as the perfect spot for a new settlement.

Inevitably, flooding has been a fact of life in Queensland's capital since the city's inception. In the 19th century, major floods in January 1841, March 1890 and February 1893 each saw the gauge top out higher than anything recorded subsequently – the 1841 flood peaked at a mind-boggling 8.43 metres, still a record. That's more than four and a half Johnathan Thurstons high.

Brisbane's 1893 disaster saw three back-to-back flood events days after two cyclones dumped more than 500 millimetres of rain on the city – half the annual average in a week. Road and rail bridges were cut, and 35 people died. During this catastrophe, subsequently described as Black February or the Great Flood, the river rose 7 metres above its ordinary level to 9.51 metres, the second highest ever recorded.

#70 We built some of our major cities in *disaster* zones.

#71 Aussies save their beer.

Described by the *Courier Mail* as the 'Long Weekend from Hell', the floods that overwhelmed Brisbane in late January 1974 were the culmination of a summer of much more southerly than normal monsoonal rains, raising watercourses to record levels across the state.

After three weeks of constant deluge, by late January almost every river in Queensland was in flood. Then a massive 642 millimetres of rain fell on Brisbane and the river's catchment area during a 36-hour period from the morning of 25 January, forcing the river over its banks.

In the worst flooding of the 20th century, the flood peaked at 6.6 metres, with the CBD badly hit. At least 6700 homes were flooded, causing damage estimated at around $200 million, and 14 lives were lost.

The *Courier Mail* reported: 'Mass evacuations were carried out, mostly in small tinnies piled with people and possessions – and often a crate of beer – labouring under outboard motors.' Those crates of beer would play a starring role in the drama.

At the peak of the inundation, brewer Castlemaine went to epic lengths to get beer safely out of the XXXX Brewery at Milton and to its customers.

'They'd made floats,' recalled packager Mr Rowbotham, who helped supply emergency boxes (the main supplier had been flooded), 'then got pallets of beer and floated them across the water to trucks waiting in the narrow lanes nearby. Brisbane was flooded … but the beer had to go.'

There's no doubt Queenslanders get their priorities right.

103

Aussies risk *death* to save others. #72

This dramatic image of Hannah Reardon-Smith and her mother Kathryn, taken on 10 January 2011, shows the life-and-death struggle people found themselves in when a flash flood hit Toowoomba in Queensland's Darling Downs region.

The previous month, December 2010, had been Queensland's wettest ever, with record high rainfall totals in 107 locations. On Christmas Day, Cyclone Tasha brought intense rainfall, swelling rivers already at capacity. Rockhampton and Bundaberg experienced their worst flooding in decades. Then, on 10 January, Toowoomba was struck by ferocious flash flooding that washed away hundreds of cars as creeks burst their banks.

In Grantham in the Lockyer Valley, houses were crushed by what the state premier described as an 'inland tsunami' of floodwaters that rose 8 metres in 30 minutes. Four people died in Toowoomba, 19 in the Lockyer Valley – 13 of whom were in their homes, hitherto considered a last refuge from disaster. One victim's body was found 80 kilometres downstream; two people listed as missing were later declared dead in June 2012, their bodies never found.

Hannah and Kathryn will always remember the bravery of Queensland Fire and Rescue station officer Peter McCarron, the third person in this picture. He entered the water to rescue the two women, who were perched on the roof of their submerged vehicle. Another car floating downstream crashed into them, sending all into the water, but both women were eventually pulled to safety.

McCarron later received a silver medal for bravery. His was among the many acts of heroism that day – 47 people were rescued by boat and 43 by helicopter – but he was dismissive of being called a hero, saying, 'I was doing my job.'

#73

One of the main crossing places on the road between Sydney and Melbourne is the town of Gundagai. Built on the banks of the Murrumbidgee River, Gundagai was settled during one of the worst droughts of the 19th century, when water levels were at historical lows. Despite warnings from the local Indigenous population about the dangers of building on river flats, Gundagai's population grew fast.

A serious flood in 1844 inundated most of the town to about a metre high and understandably freaked out inhabitants, but the governor denied a request to move the town to higher ground. On 25 June 1852, after a month of heavy rain, Gundagai was hit by Australia's most deadly flash flood.

Frightened residents climbed onto roofs to avoid being washed away in what was a massively traumatic experience. According to one survivor: 'Men, women and children never ceased screaming the whole time … A lull would come for a few moments, we could hear the most heart-rending shrieks from those who were on the top of their houses, crying for help, but none could be given them … The once happy and thriving town of Gundagai was now a desolate, wretched waste.'

At the peak of the flood, the river was 1.6 kilometres wide. Only three buildings remained standing, with 89 people dead, a

Entire towns have been swept away.

third of the population. The town was rebuilt on higher ground – this picture, taken during a later flood in 1896, shows the flood plains where the town originally sat, and the new buildings on the higher banks.

OZ FACT

Indigenous men featured prominently in the tales of rescue, coming to the aid of residents stranded on rooftops and in trees. Reports tell of one man, 'Yarri', single-handedly saving 49 people by paddling out into the raging river in a small bark canoe. Yarri and others were presented with inscribed breastplates as a token of the townsfolk's appreciation.

Entire cities

thre

Battered by its worst floods in 60 years in December 2010, Bundaberg had definitely seen enough water for a decade or two. Then in January 2013, Cyclone Oswald – one of the wettest cyclones in Queensland's history – brought severe storms and record rainfall.

On 26 January, five separate tornadoes wreaked havoc on Bundaberg before flood levels rose to the highest in the city's history, with 7500 residents evacuated.

Patients were rescued from the hospital and homeowners airlifted from their roofs by helicopter, children were pictured trying to surf in shallow water near the Bundaberg sign, and floodwaters in the Burnett River peaked at 9.52 metres, the highest level ever.

From the air, the devastation appeared total – whole suburbs were entirely underwater. More than 4000 properties were damaged, more than half left uninhabitable.

Photographer Max Fleet could not believe what he saw. 'These main streets are surreal ... It's just bizarre. Like a war zone.'

OZ FACT

Rodney Hartwig won an outstanding bravery award for his actions in saving his Bundaberg neighbour during the flood while his own house went under. As the flooded Burnett River ravaged his property at Eidsvold, Mr Hartwig, 63, attempted to save neighbour Lucy Connolly. Trying to reach her first in a ute, then a tractor in the dark, Hartwig and son Graham launched a tinny at dawn. The pair navigated the boat in half light through debris, submerged trees, livestock and power lines and finally found Ms Connolly, who had been clinging to the top of a tree for five hours.

have been
atened #74

After the flood comes the clean-up. And some unexpected guests.

While helping to clear the rubble out of destroyed homes, rescuer Dave Russo was standing in shoulder-height floodwater in the Queensland town of Gympie when he spotted this crocodile.

'What do you do?' he asks. 'You don't hang around. You get to a boat as quickly as you can and get out. You don't expect to see a croc on the pavement but nobody wants to mess with a crocodile.'

Floods, it seems, have the rather unfortunate habit of not only uprooting and displacing people, but also relocating animals from their natural environment. In the 2011 Queensland floods, approximately 1000 snakes sheltered with two owners on one isolated homestead protected from rising waters by an area of raised ground the size of a football oval.

State Disaster Coordinator (what a title!) Ian Stewart said authorities were monitoring the threat. 'We have extra vials of antivenin at the hospitals in surrounding flooded areas,' he explained. 'We've made sure we've warned communities that snakes are coming out.'

Yep, snakes on a (flood) plain – you read it here.

In 2013, snakes up to two metres long were spotted in Bundaberg's streets. 'The snakes are a massive problem. I've shut all the doors because they're coming in,' said Suzanne Miller, owner of the Pioneer Hotel pub, adding that her mother was 'almost killed' by a brown snake. 'She could feel the tongue flicking onto her face to test how far away it was, ready to bite.'

So, stressed-out snakes on the loose. Oh, and that log floating by? That's no log. '[Snakes] are very, very cranky right now,' said the State Emergency Service's Scott Mahaffey. '[And] the problem with crocodiles now is it's very, very hard to pick [them out] with the amount of debris.'

Just cos the rain has stopped doesn't mean the coast is *clear*.

#75

#76

People braving floodwaters are a little bit heroically *batshit* insane.

Aussies are nothing if not brave and ingenious. In 2015 Steve Spowart donned a wetsuit and paddled out on his surfboard to rescue horses from fast-rising floodwaters near Dungog, in New South Wales.

Some of the animals were trapped behind barbed wire, and they were getting frightened and pretty panicky. According to photographer Daniel Munoz, who shot these dramatic images, Spowart eventually led the horses to safety after cutting a gap through fencing.

'He told me that horses instinctively follow each other,' said Munoz, 'and if he could get hold of one then the others would follow.' Surfer, horse rescuer and deadset legend.

The internet is flooded with pictures of Aussies rescuing wildlife from the water. Check out Rodney Dowton ferrying a mob of wallabies across NSW's Lake Burrendong. Or Jen Lound on the same lake giving a kangaroo a lift on her kayak. During evacuations of the Daly River region in the Northern Territory, 60 animals were airlifted to safety, along with pet food.

Rolling up your sleeves and helping out a mate in need is the Australian way. Ipswich man Ray Cole was standing with his son watching the fast-moving floodwaters of Queensland's swollen Bremer River on 11 January 2011 when he spotted a distressed joey in terrible trouble. 'My son looked at me and said, "Can you save the roo, Dad?"' Mr Cole told the *Brisbane Times*.

'Before you knew it, I was neck-deep in water saving the roo. It was one of those spur-of-the-moment things; the way I was brought up … was to lend a hand if you can and it wouldn't have mattered to me whether it was a roo or a human, you know, I would have been in there.'

The photos of the heroic rescue made Mr Cole, a truck driver and father of five, a global sensation, and provided hope for decimated communities in Queensland. But Cole suffered too. Just two months later, he revealed that, like many whose lives were turned upside down by the floods,

#77
However bad things are, *someone* always gets the job done.

the experience had taken a 'severe toll' on his family's mental health. Looters destroyed his house two weeks after the flood, his wife had a breakdown and his son was hit by a truck (although fortunately survived).

'One minute I'm on the phone doing kangaroo interviews and I'm a happy chappie, you know, and then the next minute I'm sitting in the lounge room … having a little cry to myself thinking how are we going to get this family back on its feet again,' he told *the Sydney Morning Herald* in March 2011.

But, Aussie battler that he is, Cole could still see a light side. Talking of the new property the family moved to in the town of Jimboomba, he said, 'We're renting a farm out here; with 300 kangaroos in the backyard. They must think I owe them a favour.'

And people will somehow keep on *smiling* despite it all.

In July 2012 farmers Sid and Jenni Brummell were marooned in their homestead on their stricken property in Rowena in the north-west of NSW, which was surrounded by floodwaters. Their yard was full of snakes, and a tinny tied to their back deck was their only mode of transport.

'It's a bit hard to handle but we are alive – that's all that matters,' said Mrs Brummell stoically.

Fast-forward to February 2014 and the Brummells' property had become a patchwork of severe drought. With no rainfall since 25 millimetres in November of the previous year, the Brummells said this was the third worst drought they had faced since the family began farming the land more than 110 years ago.

'It's hard to believe all this was underwater,' Mrs Brummell told the *Daily Telegraph*. 'It's so dry that cracks on the ground are so deep you could lose you mobile phone.' But, she added with true Aussie fortitude, 'There's always someone worse off than you are.'

Drought to flood and back again. Australia's endless cycle of natural disasters is an intrinsic aspect of our national character, best characterised by Dorothea Mackellar's 1904 poem 'My Country'.

I love a sunburnt country,

A land of sweeping plains,

Of ragged mountain ranges,

Of droughts and flooding rains.

I love her far horizons,

I love her jewel-sea,

Her beauty and her terror –

The wide brown land for me!

STOR

Crazy-shit fan? You're in the right place. Australia is basically a batshit insaniac's heaven.

With an inherent, in-built desire to live on the edge, Aussies just love hanging out in ferocious conditions like this. For most of the year, Australia is a blue-sky country by day, boasting star-filled skies at night. More often than not, our weather can be succinctly summarised in the words of Tourism Queensland's famous slogan: 'Beautiful one day, perfect the next'.

But sometimes – well, okay, surprisingly often – this cheesy-mostly-truism could be tweaked to 'beautiful one day, completely frickin' crazy the next'.

Australia's unbelievable troika – fires, floods and storms – are fuelled by epic, swirling continental weather systems that can drop deadly serious energy and massive winds or cyclonic tempests, creating storm conditions madder than a cut snake (we have them too, remember?).

One minute you're dreamily enjoying a clear, cloudless sky. The next a storm front moves in at a breathtaking pace, dragging chaos in its wake. Whatever madness the weather brings, we know that next time, it's going be be even crazier.

While Australians treat the forces of nature with respect, a photo like this shows a fundamental Aussie trait of having a laugh in the middle of utter pandemonium. Okay, also an ability to do incredibly stupid/brave things, but you get the picture. Aussie resilience comes out in the funniest ways, not least of all in our willingness to embrace the crazy with the calm.

We have cloud tsunamis

#79
Yep.

There is something gloriously, predictably Australian about the rapidly arriving 'cool change' that brings a hot spell of weather to a ferociously dramatic end. Eastern cities appear particularly prone to such intense thunderstorms, which 99 per cent of the time seem to arrive during a sweltering afternoon when the entire city has hit the beach.

Forget days – we're talking blue skies one *minute*, monster storm the next. Tourists watch, gobsmacked and a little afraid. But defiant regulars refuse to roll up towels or retreat from the surf until the threatening formation is almost overhead. Then the iPhones come out to get the perfect shot.

These fronts are rather lazily although evocatively described on social media as 'cloud tsunamis'. More properly, they're known as shelf or arcus clouds: clearly defined wedges at the pointy end of fabulously fast-moving thunderstorms, where downdraft and updraft intersect. The result is something rare, beautiful and incredibly powerful, as this epic picture of a shelf cloud behind Sydney's Bondi Beach shows.

OZ FACT

Further north, global cloud-spotters pilgrimage to Far North Queensland every spring to catch the infamous Morning Glory, one of the world's most famous cloud formations. This magnificent, mysterious arcus roll cloud can stretch in a single band or series of bands for up to 1000 kilometres in length, roughly equivalent to the distance from Melbourne to Sydney. Of course, being Australia, just seeing this cloud isn't enough for some – Morning Glory attracts glider pilots who come to 'ride' the cloud wave.

#80

So there you are, taking in a perfectly idyllic sunset, when out of the west a monstrous cloud formation appears. This is a scenario very familiar to Brisbanites, who are blessed to live in what is not only Australia's warmest state capital but also its most thunderous.

Brissie has 33 annual 'thunder days', and when the boom hits the room it's like no bass drop you've ever heard. Intense hailstorms powered by gigantic supercells are a fact of life in south-east Queensland.

In November 2014 Brisbane was smashed by its worst hailstorm in 30 years, with chunks the size of golf balls amid wind gusts of 141 kilometres per hour leaving a trail of

Our storms have a weird habit of *creeping* up on you.

destruction and a damage bill of more than $1.3 billion.

Insurers received more than 100,000 claims for damage, including 65,000 to cars: the largest single claims event Queensland has ever seen.

'Many cars around me lost their front and rear windscreens,' reported driver Ali Cameron, whose own car was written off in the turmoil. 'I realised this storm was of a whole other level.'

OZ FACT

Storms and insurance figures make for interesting reading. From an insurance perspective, Sydney's April 1999 hailstorm was the costliest disaster in Australian history with claims exceeding $1.7 billion. The storm was said to have shot down more than 500,000 tonnes of hailstones, some as big as cricket balls. What is it with Aussies comparing hailstones and balls, we ask? Well, we are a sports-loving nation, and any chance to merge that with a little friendly 'it was that big' reference can't be overlooked.

No doubt you've heard the age-old rhyme 'Red sky at night, sailors' delight./Red sky at morning, sailors take warning'. Cute, catchy, and probably very useful. Unless you're in Australia.

Tugboat worker Brett Martin and his mates were out in the ocean off Onslow, in the Pilbara region of Western Australia, on 9 January 2013 when they spotted a spectacular storm whipping itself into something they'd never seen.

'We were steaming along in the boat just before sunset and the storm was casually building in the distance,' Martin told the *West Australian*. 'Then it got faster and faster and it went from glass to about 40 knots in two minutes. It was like a big dust storm under a thunderhead; there was a lot of lightning but not a lot of rain.'

Arriving just before a tropical cyclone, the storm picked up huge amounts of red dust and iron ore from the nearby Pilbara region and then built up into a towering wall that dwarfed nearby ships and reduced visibility to 100 metres.

There's no such thing as a 'normal day' on the *water*.

#81

117

There's no such thing as a 'normal day' on *land*.

#82

That red Australian topsoil can really create a scene, as this picture from Nain, in South Australia's Barossa Valley region, shows.

On 17 March 2016, rolling walls of the stuff were whipped up by strong winds, causing serious visibility problems. 'I could barely see 20 metres in front of me,' said one resident.

In one of those tragic Australian double-whammies, much of the dust was lifted from the soil left exposed after the Pinery bushfire, a devastating blaze that swept

through the region in November 2015, destroying 91 homes and claiming two lives.

Local Charmaine Holland said that seeing the dust storm approach was like 'déjà vu' after the Pinery fire, in which her home was ravaged. 'Everything was going blood red … We had so many dust storms here in the last months it's not funny.'

Dust storms are a fairly common sight in Australia, although no less shocking for that fact. What's extra freaky is that their colour conjures up thoughts of unbearable heat yet dust storms are associated with cold fronts.

A scene from *Independence Day*? Nah, just another freaky storm day in the Land Down Under.

When Australia's thunderstorms come a-calling, they really unleash. This image shows lightning strikes over Sydney during a particularly incredible storm at the end of a humid day on 3 December 2014. The image is cleverly time-lapse stacked, showing all the strikes photographer Roland Taylor captured in 20 minutes while shooting the storm from his apartment balcony in Surry Hills.

So, how likely are you to be hit by lightning in Australia? According to much-loved Aussie scientist Dr Karl Kruszelnicki, there are about 100 lightning bolts every second around the world that result in 'only' 100 deaths per year: 'So your odds are very, very good.' The safest place to be? Inside your car, which acts as a lightning conductor. The most dangerous place? Under a tree. Golfers, beware!

'A tree is God's natural lightning conductor,' explains Dr Karl. 'The sap in the trunk can boil instantly and explode with a force of a quarter of a tonne. About one quarter of all people killed by lightning were hiding under a tree.'

Okay, tree, we get it. And if you're out in the open in a storm and feel the hairs on your skin stand on end, DO NOT lie down on the ground, which only increases danger. When lightning strikes the ground, it branches out. To reduce the chances of being struck, you need to minimise your *height* and your body's contact with the Earth's surface. Or just stay indoors.

OZ FACT

At least 650 Australians have been killed by lightning strikes since records began, with the peak months coinciding with summer, and males under 35 the biggest group at risk.

#83 Lightning turns Aussie skies into a *sci-fi* movie.

Some days you just feel as if the *apocalyp* has arrived.

#84

Armageddon? Apocalypse? Mars? Sydney.

On 23 September 2009, the harbour city woke up to one of the weirdest sights it had ever seen – a creepy, low-visibility 'red dawn' caused by the biggest dust storm to hit Sydney since records began. Carried by gale-force winds of up to 100 kilometres per hour, an estimated 16 million tonnes of desert dust had been picked up thousands of kilometres inland in the drought-baked Lake Eyre.

Sydney Airport was closed, ferry services cancelled and children kept at home as city pharmacies quickly sold out of face masks and respiratory medication.

OZ FACT

Funnily enough, something so red had one very green outcome: dropping iron-rich dust on the ocean, the storm apparently triggered a bloom in phytoplankton, tiny organisms that serve as the basis for much of the ocean's food chains.

Callers to talkback radio asked if North Korea had launched an attack. 'It's like a nuclear winter morning,' tourist Peter Wilson told Reuters. 'It is so eerie.'

On route to Sydney the day before, the storm had hit Broken Hill, where residents used wet rolled-up towels to plug the gaps under doors.

'It was absolutely pitch black: you couldn't even see your hand in front of you,' Doug Banks told *Australian Geographic*. 'Headlights couldn't illuminate anything because it was like they were shining off a solid wall of dirt.'

The dust storm was huge: 'Ten very dry years over inland southern Australia and very strong westerlies have conspired to produce these storms,' explained Nigel Tapper, environmental scientist at Monash University.

It's pretty much the wildest video you'll ever see: a car suddenly emerging from head-high foam at Mooloolaba on Queensland's Sunshine Coast, almost taking out two police officers who were directing traffic.

'It was a shock to everyone,' local Michael Bell told the *Courier Mail* after capturing the chaos on film. 'I showed the footage to the two officers and the one who pushed the other out of the way thought he was pretty famous.'

Big waves and rough seas in the wake of Cyclone Oswald in January 2013 created freak foam conditions that became a tourist attraction in their own right. The frothy brew

swept across the beach, into holiday resorts and people's homes. Caravans at a low-lying holiday park were totally inundated, and thousands of Queenslanders flocked to see the salty 'winter wonderland'.

But just because it's fluffy doesn't mean it's fun. After holidaymakers at Mooloolaba Beach Holiday Park complained of itching and stinging, a University of Queensland toxicologist warned of hidden dangers lurking within the foam, telling the *Sunshine Coast Daily* that residents should steer clear for fears it could be poisonous and contain pollutants, toxins and sewage. (Note to self: foam bad.)

Local kids, on the other hand, were all, like, 'YOLO!'

#85
Beaches of f*cking *foam*? What is wrong with you, Australia?!

> **OZ FACT**
> Sea-foam forms when natural detergent-like chemicals from phytoplankton bloom or seaweed that normally sits in the microlayer of the ocean surface is whipped into a foamy mass by big seas. Or maybe that giant squid just forgot to turn off the washing machine.

Smashing into the Queensland coast near Mission Beach on 3 February 2011, with wind speeds of 295 kilometres per hour, category 5 Cyclone Yasi was almost as big as North America (the image above shows Yasi atop the map) and more powerful than Hurricane Katrina, which hit New Orleans in 2005, killing at least 1245 people.

Facing one of Australia's biggest storms ever, authorities moved 30,000 residents inland from their beachfront properties and evacuated Cairns Base Hospital before Yasi touched down.

Forecasters hardly slept for five days as the storm approached, busy preparing their own families and homes for the disaster. They breathed a sigh of relief in the final few hours when it became obvious that the cyclone was going to hit the coast south of Cairns.

'There was a lot of apprehension,' recalled Bureau of Meteorology forecaster Bill O'Connor. 'If it did track 150 kilometres north, there would have been a lot more damage to the city of Cairns.'

But residents of Cardwell, Tully and Mission Beach weren't so lucky, enduring a horrific night bunkered down before dawn revealed 'scenes of mass devastation'.

At Port Hinchinbrook marina, Yasi caused total carnage, transforming the millionaires' playground into a wrecking yard, with 56 boats piled up by the 7-metre storm surge. Offshore, the luxury resort at Dunk Island was destroyed beyond recognition, its stunning pool completely filled with sand. Miraculously, mass evacuations had prevented major loss of life.

#86

Australian storms are big. VERY big indeed.

OZ FACT

The costliest cyclone ever to hit Australia, Yasi caused $3.6 billion worth of damage, ravaging homes and banana and sugar crops. It didn't disperse until it hit Uluru in the Red Centre.

Aussies aren't going to let a little thing like a *cyclone* ruin their day. #87

When super-intense, super-powerful Cyclone Tracy devastated Darwin early on Christmas Day of 1974 it took the city totally by surprise, killing 66 people and leaving 41,000 homeless.

More than 70 per cent of homes were destroyed and communication, power and water were severed.

As news filtered through to the rest of Australia, authorities announced that 'Darwin had, for the time being, ceased to exist as a city'.

The entire RAAF fleet of transport planes and 13 navy ships were deployed to help, and within four days 35,000 people had been evacuated.

Shocked and saddened, Australia rushed to help, with PM Gough Whitlam promising residents 'a determined and unremitting effort to rebuild your city'. Locals displayed their own unique resilience – graffiti daubed on the back of ruined cars ('Tracy You Bitch') and outside destroyed cinemas ('Now Showing: *Gone with the Wind*, starring Cyclone Tracy') captured the city's defiant humour in the face of disaster.

This photo of three-year-old Poppy Magoulis (now Papazoglou) is a moving image of innocence amid the destruction. Today, the mother of three doesn't recall the picture being taken but does remember waiting out the cyclone with her family inside their house.

Later in the day, Poppy and her mother went outside to check on some neighbours. 'Mum said I just saw the tricycle there and jumped on it and started riding around.'

By 1978 Darwin returned to its pre-Tracy population – today, 115,000 Darwinians battle crocs, cyclones and average annual highs of 33°C to show that, whatever Mother Nature throws at us, Aussies will batten down the hatches, then pick ourselves up, get back on the bike and get ready to rebuild.

Hope you enjoyed this little tour of Australia. Oh, but one last thing: don't brush against the trees as you go. Cos you could, you know, die.

The Gympie-Gympie stinging tree is one of four species of stinging trees in Australia, and, natch, one of the most venomous plants in the world. Its sting is delivered via tiny silicon hairs that cover the leaves and fruit. These hairs penetrate your skin, break off and show no sign of leaving you. Next stop, anaphylactic shock.

Entomologist and ecologist Marina Hurley was a postgrad student at James Cook University when she spent three years studying these fierce flora in Queensland's Atherton Tableland (the trees are most commonly found in Australia's tropics).

Her first encounter produced a sneezing fit and left her eyes and nose running for hours. Then came the inevitable stings, one of which saw her hospitalised.

'Being stung is the worst kind of pain you can imagine,' recalls Hurley, 'like being burnt with hot acid and electrocuted at the same time.'

And that was before the allergic reaction, which developed over time. 'At that point my doctor advised that I should have no further contact with the plant and I didn't object.'

It's typical, isn't it? If the creepy-crawlies, feral beasts and unbelievable natural disasters don't get you, our foliage will.

Oh well, if you don't like it, just make like a tree and leave.

BEWARE STINGING TREE

VISITORS ARE ADVISED TO BEWARE OF THE STINGING TREE. CONTACT CAN CAUSE SEVERE PAIN AND DISTRESS. IF STUNG - SEEK IMMEDIATE MEDICAL ATTENTION ..... DIAL 000

危険　スティンギグーツリーにご注意！

この辺りには、スティングツリーがございます。トゲに刺されると激痛を引き起こしますのでご注意下さい。万一、刺された場合は直ぐに治療を受けてください。

救急電話番号 000

Because *OUCH.*

Having nightmares?

If you've got this far you've almost certainly concluded that Australia is a godforsaken hell hole that no sensible person should ever visit, and that all residents should leave. But of course, in reality Australia is basically heaven on Earth, and we just make this stuff up to keep the beaches empty.

OR DO WE?!

Acknowledgements

Picture credits

Page 2, Shutterstock.com / sciencepics;
pp 4–5 (crocodile), Shutterstock.com / jantima14;
pp 4–5 (sign), Shutterstock.com / Lorimer Images;
p 7, Jacob Brant / NT News Facebook; p 8, Matt Wright;
p 10, Newspix; p 11, Sandra Bell; p 12, Shutterstock.com; p 13, Chris Keeping; p 14, Newspix / Michael Franchi; p 15, photo by Australia Zoo via Getty Images;
p 16, Alamy / Madeleine Hall; p 17, Newspix / Doron Aviguy; p 19, Brian Cassey; p 20, Danielle Haynes;
p 21, Peter Collins / Broome Bird Observatory;
p 23, Marvin Muller; p 24, Jody / ABC Far North Queensland; p 25, Elliot Budd; p 26, via Bryan Robinson;
p 27, AAP Image / AP Photo / Queensland Police;
p 28, Robert Weber; p 29, Queensland Police Service;
p 31, Jurgen Otto; p 32, Claire McFarlane;
p 33, leokimv7ideo / YouTube; p 34, Patrick Futcher;
p 35, Michael Doe; p 36, Dean Osland; p 38, Auscape / Densey Clyne; p 39, AAP Image / Lukas Coch;
p 40, Wikimedia Commons / Calistemon (CC BY-SA 3.0);
p 41, Newspix / Les Martin; p 42, Shutterstock.com;
p 44, Shutterstock.com; p 45, Getty Images / Awashima Marine Park; p 46, Newspix / Jodie Richter; p 47, Newspix / Peter Lorimer; p 48, Alamy / Jeff Rotman; p 49, Max Muggeridge / TBD Sharkfishing; p 50, AAP Image/AP Photo/Sea Shepherd; p 51, Shutterstock.com;
p 52, AAP Image/ Tammy Ven Dange; p 54, Chris 'Brolga' Barns / Kangaroo Sanctuary; p 55, Faye Bedford;
p 56, Fairfax / Darren Pateman; p 58, Newspix / Adam Taylor; p 59, Shutterstock.com / Johan Larson;
p 60, Eivind Undheim; p 62, Ajay Narenda / Macquarie University; p 63, Shutterstock.com / PAPound;
p 65, Alamy / Rob Walls; p 66, Getty Images / Paul Sutherland; p 68, AAP Image / Lloyd Jones; p 69, Hal Cogger; p 71, Shutterstock.com / Yusran Abdul Rahman;
p 72, Getty Images / Franco Banfi; p 73, Shutterstock.com / Yongkiet Jitwattanatam; p 74 (l), Genevieve Di Carlo; p 74 (r), Sharon Scoble; p 75, Newspix; p 77, Getty Images / Minden Pictures / Michael and Patricia Fogden;

p 78, Caroline Brocx / InTheBush; p 79, Robert Lang;
p 80, Hap Cameron; p 81, Main Roads Western Australia;
p 82, Shutterstock.com / totajla; p 84, Shutterstock.com / Robert Paul van Beets; p 85, Shutterstock.com / Neale Cousland; p 86, Flickr / AJ Oswald (detail) (CC BY-SA 2.0);
p 87, Getty Images / Quinn Rooney; p 89, Paul Walker;
p 90, CSIRO ScienceImage (detail of DA0063) (CC BY 3.0); p 91, National Library of Australia (nla.obj-138501179); p 92, Fairfax; p 93, Fairfax; p 94, AAP Image / AP / Mark Parden; p 96, AAP Image / Andrew Brownbill; p 97, Chris Tangey / Alice Springs Film & TV; p 98, Getty Images / Daniel Berehulak;
p 99, Shutterstock.com / Istimages; p 101, Getty Images / Chris Hyde; p 102, Getty Images / AFP / Torsten Blackwood; p 103, Newspix; p 104, Toowoomba Chronicle / Nev Madsen; p 105, Gormly Family Collection RW98/25, Charles Sturt University Regional Archives;
p 107, Paul Beutel; p 108, Daily Mail Australia;
p 109, Getty Images / Daniel Munoz; p 110, Nick de Villiers; p 111, Newspix / Peter Lorimer; p 113, Getty Images / Brendan Thorne; p 114, Shutterstock.com;
p 116, Jacob Lambert; p 117, Brett Martin and Perth Weather Live; p 118, Charmaine Holland; p 119, Roland Taylor; p 121, Getty Images / Cameron Spencer;
p 122, Getty Images / Chris Hyde; p 123 (l), NOAA / NASA Blue Marble; p 123 (r), Newspix / Evan Morgan;
p 124, Newspix / Bruce Howard; p 125, Flickr / Michael Coghlan (CC BY-SA 2.0) (detail); p 126, Brian Cassey.

NOTE: While efforts have been made to trace and acknowledge all copyright holders, in some cases this has been unsuccessful. If you believe you hold copyright in a photograph, please contact the publisher.

Poetry extract
Extract from 'My Country' by Dorothea Mackellar on p 111 by arrangement with the Licensor, The Dorothea Mackellar Estate, c/- Curtis Brown (Aust) Pty Ltd

The ABC 'Wave' device is a trademark of the Australian Broadcasting Corporation and is used under licence by HarperCollinsPublishers Australia.

First published in Australia in 2016
by HarperCollinsPublishers Australia Pty Limited
ABN 36 009 913 517
harpercollins.com.au

HarperCollinsPublishers
Level 13, 201 Elizabeth Street, Sydney, NSW 2000, Australia
Unit D1, 63 Apollo Drive, Rosedale, Auckland 0632, New Zealand
A 53, Sector 57, Noida, UP, India
1 London Bridge Street, London, SE1 9GF, United Kingdom
2 Bloor Street East, 20th floor, Toronto, Ontario M4W 1A8, Canada
195 Broadway, New York, NY 10007

National Library of Australia Cataloguing-in-Publication data:

Crerar, Simon, author.

88 reasons why Australia is the craziest / Simon Crerar, BuzzFeed.

ISBN: 9780733335693 (paperback)

Subjects: Curiosities and wonders – Australia

Australia – Miscellanea

Other Creators/Contributors: BuzzFeed, author.

994

Cover and internal design by bookdesignbysaso.com.au
Front cover image by The Kangaroo Sanctuary, Alice Springs
Back cover images by Michael Doe (spider); Eivind Undheim (centipede);
and shutterstock.com (crocodile).
Typeset in ITC Franklin Gothic LT
Printed and bound in China by RR Donnelley

The papers used by HarperCollins in the manufacture of this book are natural, recyclable product made from wood grown in sustainable plantation forests. The fibre source and manufacturing processes meet recognised international environmental standards, and carry certification.